SHARK
HEART

A LOVE STORY

Emily Habeck is an alumna of SMU's Meadows School of the Arts, where she received a BFA in theatre, as well as Vanderbilt Divinity School and Vanderbilt's Peabody College. She is from Ardmore, Oklahoma. *Shark Heart* is her first novel.

SHARK
HEART

A LOVE STORY

Emily Habeck

Jo Fletcher
BOOKS

First published in Great Britain in 2023

Jo Fletcher Books
An imprint of
Quercus Editions Ltd
Carmelite House
50 Victoria Embankment
London EC4Y 0DZ

An Hachette UK company

A CIP catalogue record for this book is available
from the British Library

ISBN 978 1 52943 221 3
Tpb ISBN 978 1 5293 222 0
Ebook ISBN 978 1 52943 224 4

10 9 8 7 6 5 4 3 2 1

Typeset by Jouve (UK), Milton Keynes

Printed and bound in Great Britain by Clays Ltd, Elcograf S.p.A.

Papers used by Jo Fletcher Books are from well-managed forests and other responsible sources.

For my parents

SHARK
HEART

SCENE ONE

LEWIS: In the early days after I left New York, I would ruminate, doubt all my choices. But when I met you, I began to thank my failure. Maybe failing was a kind of miracle. Maybe everything happened just right.

WREN: You are an excellent teacher. You've said so yourself: everything in New York led you to what you should have been doing all along if you weren't so stubborn. And you're still so young. You can do anything. You can act, perform in plays again, if you want. I could support us if you want to try again.

LEWIS: Thank you, but that's not what— I,
    I am saying the wrong things.
    I'm talking too much about myself.
    What my point is, what I'm getting at is:
    My failure as an artist led me to you,
    with your bird wrists, twig fingers,
    you, with your efficient days
    making lists
    researching
    you, who can make a spreadsheet
    about almost anything.
    You make everything better than when you found it,
    even me.

LEWIS (*continued*): Will you let me stand beside you on your plot of earth? We'll tell the weeds to grow tall around our ankles, and when the wind gives us sycamore seeds, we'll raise them as sprouts, seedlings, saplings until they overpower, shade, and nurture us. Our trees will grow for two hundred years or more as our union becomes even more unquestionable and strong. Unquestionable because no one will remember a time when we were not creating our universe. Strong because trees two hundred years old have been great witnesses to it all. Then, one day, we'll die gladly into the soil we shared, and fungi will take over what was once our bodies. Bouquets of mushrooms, little families, will mark the place of our lives.

To be of the ground is to be of life.

You taught me that.

You,

a woman whose deepest belly laugh makes no sound

a woman who notices every detail

a woman made of a brilliance you don't see

no matter how many times I show you.

Sometimes I wonder if you might not be a person at all,

but a spirit

or a fairy

or a memory,

and I'm watching *Good Morning America* in a hospital room or a prison, or maybe this is all the most wonderful, strange dream. I don't want to wake up. I like to think we met in a daydream once, a long time ago, and decided to meet right here, right now. Wren, you are the most complicated person I have ever known. I mean—in the best way, complicated, and somehow terrifically unaffected by fragile things like youth, beauty, promises, and dreams, and I want to keep on knowing you—well, trying to—all the days of my life. So, I want to ask you: Will you marry me, Wren? Will you be my wife?

Wren was unlike any woman Lewis had ever met. She presented herself just as she was from the beginning, consistent and clear. No tricks, secrets, or games. Wren did not love him obliquely, making him dance for her affection.

She divided every dinner receipt to the cent and never left a trace of herself at his apartment. Early was on time. She found spontaneity stressful. She did not like the sound of flowery words or the weight of gift boxes. She was five steps ahead. She took notes. She scanned every environment for trouble, hypervigilant. She did not watch television to be entertained but to realize the ending before it happened. Wren would say *I love you*, but she almost cringed to hear it in return.

Unlike Lewis, Wren did not take life personally or let her feelings run wild. Wren's love was true but methodical, and for the first time in all his life, Lewis felt secure and accepting of his sensitivity and inner turbulence, because Wren loved him just as he was.

Wren's skill as a listener endeared her to everyone they knew. She remembered everything anyone ever said to her. As a conversationalist, Wren asked questions that were specific but never invasive. When asked of her own life, however, she gave simple, generic answers. There was never much to say about herself. Wren let others take up all the space they needed, because she was always doing just fine.

Lewis used to miss the activities he shared with the artistically motivated women from his past—drinking cheap wine until two o'clock in the morning, talking about old films, going to warehouse plays, giving notes on screenplays, and comforting each other after a horrible audition.

As their relationship became more committed, deep, and real, Lewis realized Wren's gift: she would never compete with him as an artist. Now he could relax and enjoy the pleasure of never having to defend his taste.

All the art he shared with Wren was an education to her, and in her unknowing, Lewis found her rarest vulnerability. Wren did not know theater, film, music, or poetry. She did not contemplate the definition of beauty or philosophize about the nature of ideas. She had never wept at an opera in another language or stood in front of a painting for an hour as a creative exercise to see what emerged from an image when one stopped trying to know it.

Wren became soft and young when she was learning, and in these moments, Lewis pretended they'd gone back in time together. On this imagined plane, Lewis and Wren were sixteen years old, discovering new music and spiraling into the sort of cloudless love that fears no consequences.

Wren grew to appreciate what Lewis loved, but she never became passionate about art herself. She let Lewis play that part, alone.

APRIL

Their wedding was intimate and lovely but practical, just like their relationship, which had never been an inferno of public passion or an opulent, material display of caring.

Wren liked quiet structured evenings with a few friends. Lewis liked boisterous gatherings where many people were invited to come and go. They settled in the middle: a ceremony in his parents' backyard with forty-four guests and a catered BBQ reception.

Since she was a teenager, Wren had only ever had herself. So it made sense that she would be the one to give herself away. A student from the high school where Lewis was a teacher played the violin as Wren came down the aisle.

What moved Lewis to tears in this moment was not the sight of Wren wearing a dress as blue as the Texas sky, his mother clutching her heart, or all the people he loved in the same place but, rather, his remembrance of the trees standing tall behind him. Lit up with string lights for the ceremony, the four live oaks were the main venue for his boyhood imagination. Lewis and those trees grew up together. And now the same trees were his best men, watching and witnessing the life he continued to create. Lewis was overwhelmed.

He'd tried to imagine this moment as a younger man, seeing the mysterious idea of his wife coming toward him down the aisle. *Who will she be?* he'd wondered for years. Now Lewis could finally answer his younger self's question: *Wren! Wren is my wife!* He exclaimed in his mind, the mystery revealed.

As Lewis held Wren's hands, he thought of her kindness, her intelligence, her inner beauty. Yet, just as he married these known qualities, he also married her vast unknowns. And she, his.

At the end of the ceremony, Lewis and Wren turned to face family and friends, a microcosm of the world who had just witnessed the transfiguration, a microcosm knowing full well that even the most beautiful marriages will bear the weight of challenge one day. But for an evening, the challenge was hypothetical; for an evening, Wren and Lewis were the lucky ones. It was their time to be happy.

They would own the future together now.

Lewis and Wren spent their wedding night at a bed-and-breakfast nestled in a field of Texas bluebonnets just outside Fort Worth. They split a gargantuan caramel pecan sticky bun and dreamed about their summer honeymoon in France. They would have gone directly after the wedding, but Lewis was about to go into tech rehearsals for the spring musical, *Sweeney Todd*, and couldn't leave town with the machine of an elaborate high school musical on his shoulders.

They both wanted to discard the pressure of making their wedding night the most romantic night of their lives, so the evening took on the cadence of any other relaxing Saturday night they would spend together. And that was a lovely thing, too.

When Lewis started dancing around the room, singing "The Worst Pies in London" in a very committed falsetto, Wren laughed until she snorted. Then, embarrassed, she apologized. Even in joy, Wren was careful and restrained.

MAY

A few weeks after the wedding, Lewis noticed something odd. The bridge of his nose was no longer a triangle of bone but, rather, soft cartilage.

Lewis was startled and concerned until he remembered hearing somewhere that one's nose and ears continued to grow throughout life. His late grandfathers each had had enormous noses and ears. *That must be the reason. My nose is growing,* Lewis thought. Then he became freshly distraught by the fact that he would be forty in a few years. *FORTY! And I've done nothing! I know nothing!* He forgot all about noses.

A week later, though, Lewis's nose was completely cartilaginous. It looked normal, but he could flatten it with his hand and press it flush against his cheeks. When he shook his head hard, his nose jiggled, like he was made of rubber. He showed Wren this new feature as if it were a party trick. But she was horrified.

"Lewis! It isn't funny! This could be a serious medical condition. You need to see a doctor."

Wren wanted to drive him to the emergency room, but Lewis calmed her by insisting he was not in pain; he promised to call Dr. Anderson in the morning.

Dr. Anderson had been Lewis's doctor since childhood and was a family friend. Lewis expected Dr. Anderson's usual jovial, joking bedside manner, but instead, he expressed deep concern, like Wren. As a nurse drew Lewis's blood, Dr. Anderson wrote down two numbers, for a rheumatologist and a neurologist.

"If you tell their offices I sent you, they'll work you in quickly. And Lewis: you do need to be seen. Quickly."

At work, Lewis was met with a jubilant theater program, glowing after a glorious run of *Sweeney Todd*. Dr. Anderson and the ominous appointment faded from his mind. With only two weeks of school left, Lewis let his classes order pizza and sing karaoke. He turned his head the other way when a group started playing the dirty version of Cards Against Humanity, but when four senior guys climbed onto the roof, Lewis put his foot down, winkingly threatening to report them to the principal's office.

"What did Dr. Anderson say?" Wren asked before she'd even taken off her blazer that evening.

"He didn't know."

"What do you mean, he didn't know?"

"He referred me to a couple specialists. I've already made the appointments," Lewis said, expecting Wren to be satisfied. Instead, she was just more inquisitive.

"What kind of specialists?"

"I don't remember."

"When are the appointments?"

"Why so many questions?"

"Because I'm worried. Aren't you worried?"

"No," Lewis said, wrapping his arms around her. "I'm young. I'm healthy. I'm not worried at all."

But Lewis wasn't being honest; he was worried. Whatever was happening to him was coming on fast. He felt thirsty all the time, and even though he drank a couple gallons of water a day, Lewis hardly urinated. Furthermore, his molars were loose, a sensation he had not experienced since childhood. As in childhood, he could feel new teeth coming in beneath the old ones, but these new teeth were not square and blunt. They were sharp, like the end of a knife.

The skin texture on Lewis's lower back and feet was the most peculiar development of all. When the affected skin became wet in the shower, it felt smooth when he stroked downward, but if he moved his hand in the opposite direction, the skin felt rough, like sandpaper. Throughout the day, the soles of his feet would become very dry. Once, his right heel even split and bled into his shoe. So he started applying a thick coat of petroleum jelly before putting on his socks each morning, and in minutes, his skin absorbed it as the healing force battled the destructive one.

Lewis's other symptoms included an increased appetite, a throbbing ache deep within his thigh and calf bones, a decrease in focus, an increase in aggression and irritability, and flashes of strong apathy. He recited this list to doctors and nurses until it was a dull, rote monologue.

And then Lewis had other concerns he could not quite articulate to the doctors. He felt different in space, nimble and buoyant, as if he were floating, not walking. Lewis could sprint without feeling his heart race. Looking into the backyard at night, he realized he saw objects more clearly than in the day. Lewis had a new awareness of sound, too, and a sensitivity to peripheral objects moving through space. He could predict someone's movements before they made them.

On the first Friday of the students' summer vacation, Lewis sat alone in his office, surrounded by plays he might select for the fall, when his phone rang.

"This is Carla from Dr. Ramirez's office calling for Lewis Woodard."

Lewis had feigned unconcern when Wren had asked if he'd gotten a call from the neurologist, but now he could not deny his anxiety. His hands trembled as he brought the phone closer to his face.

"This is Lewis Woodard speaking," he replied in a voice deeper than his natural one.

"Hi, Mr. Woodard. I'm calling to let you know we have the results of the tests. Dr. Ramirez would like you to come in to discuss them."

"Can you also tell me now?"

"I'm sorry. Dr. Ramirez would like to see you in person."

Two days later, Dr. Ramirez sat before him, clasping his hands and leaning forward, like a preacher.

"We finally have everything back from the lab. The diagnosis is very clear," Dr. Ramirez said briskly to mask the gravity of what came next. "You're in the early stages of a Carcharodon carcharias mutation."

"Carcharo— What?"

. . .

"Carcharodon carcharias. Great white shark."

Lewis felt dizzy and wished he had brought Wren to the appointment. He hadn't because, through all of this, he did not want to cause worry if it was nothing. But it wasn't nothing. His diagnosis was very much something. Lewis heard only snippets:

"Chondrichthyes mutations, what we call the class of cartilaginous fish mutations, are usually fast-developing, aggressive. We don't currently have a way to ease the transition between air and water breathing. Some patients report a sensation of constant suffocation toward the end . . .

10

"Some maintain a few human features at the time of release, but these features do resolve in time. Patients typically continue to develop after being released in the ocean . . .

"I looked over your MRI, and your ankles, knees, hips, and elbows are almost completely cartilage. I'm surprised you're still walking. How is the pain?"

As Lewis hobbled to his car with a few pamphlets and seven prescriptions to pick up after work, he tried to remember all Dr. Ramirez had said and regretted not writing some things down. He could not even pronounce the name of the diagnosis. He would just have to look everything up on the Internet later.

Lewis decided to keep his bad news private, separate from his daily life, for as long as he could. He pretended that avoidance would diminish his symptoms and make the whole ordeal unreal. But as the existing symptoms intensified and new ones emerged, the secret itself had almost as many symptoms as the disease. He knew he had to tell Wren. Soon.

Meanwhile, she kept hammering him with questions: *Has Dr. Ramirez called today? Maybe you should follow up. Why don't you just check in with the nurse? Didn't they say they would know in about a week? I think they sometimes forget to call. Maybe they sent you an email. Did you check your spam? Maybe they posted something on the patient portal. Do you remember making a password?*

Then Lewis's secret became an outright lie.

When he was alone, Lewis's mind raced.

When he was with others, Lewis pretended everything was fine.

When he was with Wren, Lewis played a characterized version of himself, punching up his idealism, sense of humor, and creative energy.

He had been an actor, after all.

Lewis often told his students that living itself could be an art form. So it made sense that his life, as their teacher, would be a demonstration of this principle. If this was Act One, Lewis still had control. He could still direct his own story.

What happened after intermission would be in nature and God's hands, if there was a god. And if there wasn't, Lewis would blame life, the chaos, the living drama.

PART ONE

WREN and LEWIS

MAIN CHARACTERS

WREN: Woman, age 35. Listener. List maker. Timekeeper. Strives to control the course of events with illusions and intangibles: willpower, pragmatism, hope, and love.

LEWIS: Man, age 35. Theater teacher. Treehouse dreamer. Director. Playwright. Failed actor, that is, until now, the performance of his lifetime.

TINY PREGNANT WOMAN: Former prodigy. Misanthrope. Mother of birds.

SETTING

Dallas, Texas. 2016.

When Wren was in elementary school, the class attached paper wishes to the dream catchers they made with yarn and disposable plates. In thick marker, Wren wrote her dream:

A Medium-Sized Life.

Second-grade Wren's reasoning was that a life too noticeable might be stolen, and conversely, a wispy existence might blow away or be stepped on. Medium was safe.

Wren's teacher, who wrote secret poetry on the weekend, found this sentiment lovely, wise, and replete rather than an indicator that a child was already carrying too much of the world.

In middle school, another teacher complimented Wren on her Quiet Confidence, and for the rest of her life, she would wear the phrase as an inner badge.

By the time Wren was thirty years old, her dream of a Medium-Sized Life was fully formed.

Her routine was even, predictable, and managed. She would do almost anything to protect her ordinariness. She was attractive but abhorred spending time in front of the mirror. She made money but avoided spending beyond the necessities. She never traveled. Some might consider Wren's life boring, but boring missed the point. She was unshakable.

In the beginning, when they were new to each other, Lewis told her often:

"You're so beautiful, you know?"

"No."

"You are."

"No."

"You are."

"Please. Stop."

"You are."

"Beauty is not important."

Lewis started to laugh, thinking Wren was joking. She wasn't.

"You're beautiful, and I'm going to tell you all the time."

"Stop the car. I want to walk home," she snapped.

"Wait—are you serious?"

"*Yes.*"

"Why?"

"Because you're not listening to me."

"I'm not allowed to shower my girlfriend with saccharine praise?"

"Exactly."

Lewis learned he had to step lightly when he showed Wren his heart. Because Lewis was a man of enormous feeling, this was the most challenging part of their relationship. But as he learned more about Wren and her past, Lewis realized her fear of vulnerability had a source.

In his own, different way, Lewis understood this kind of resistance well.

All his life, Lewis wanted to be an actor on the professional stage. (*On Broadway!* Part of him still wanted it so much he could barely say it.) His relationship with theater was beyond passion: it was his calling.

He loved the institution of the theater as if it were a god, and acting his religion, but the theater had not loved him back. In fact, it never even let him inside except as an outsider, an admirer, an audience member, a student. From Lewis, the theater only took, took, took, took; it took his twenties and his fire; it took his money and his time.

On a Sunday-afternoon walk around White Rock Lake their first November, Wren told Lewis the story of her mother, Angela, in a detached yet transparent way. (Much later, Lewis would realize how much courage it took for Wren to share this part of herself.)

Wren's mother nurtured and raised her, but at a certain point in her childhood, Wren had to nurture and raise her mother. Angela gave Wren a life and home but also took her childhood and innocence; her curiosity and flexibility; her imagination and wonder. Sometimes Wren said she resented her mother, and other times Wren missed her so much it was hard to move, to breathe.

Lewis's solar plexus tingled with recognition, because beneath the superficial differences in their personalities, occupations, tax brackets, and lived experiences, they were the same—overworked and abandoned by what they dearly, desperately loved.

When Wren was eighteen, she chose a college in New England, because she wanted to get far away from Oklahoma. After college, she accepted a job at a private equity firm and moved to Boston. She lasted just under two years in the job before deciding to move closer to home.

In the years Wren was away, she gradually felt two things at once. One, she was grateful to be, at last, away from Oklahoma with a fresh start. Two, something about the Northeast did not feel like home.

Wren disliked the ceiling of gray, the hungry, gaping mouth of seasonal depression that seemed to swallow her from October until April. She also thought the high cost of living was not justified by a place so crowded and cold. In contrast, Oklahoma and the region she loathed as an adolescent now seemed vivid, spacious, and welcoming.

She missed the illusion of grass and sky kissing at the end of the world. She missed standing amid a rustling chorus of wind-waving grasses, the four horsemen of the tallgrass prairie—little bluestem, big bluestem, Indian grass, and switchgrass. She missed May fields dotted with black-eyed Susans, Indian blanket, and coreopsis. She missed bursts of red clay topsoil along dirt roads. She missed the smell emanating from meat smokers, the way the grocery store was always empty on Sunday mornings, good thirty-dollar haircuts, and scissor-tailed flycatchers, suspended like supermen in hot, dry air. She missed the evenings most of all: the grapefruit sun hovering above the prairie, dismissing the day with unpredictable strokes of cantaloupe, fuchsia, and violet.

It was as if her psyche contained a magnet that activated its pull only when she was away from the Great Plains and her mother.

Dallas appealed to Wren for the reasons some people disliked it. At first glance unspecialized, covered with characterless concrete, flat, and landlocked, the city felt big enough to disappear in but not big enough to get lost in. It mirrored a quality of emotionlessness Wren tried to embody herself. People were nice enough. She was close enough to her mother's facility to drive up with a few hours' notice.

Wren and Lewis first met at a popular café on Elm Street with a big patio. It was a beautiful fall day in 2012, the Saturday before Obama was elected to a second term.

Lewis was on a date with a woman whose vinelike legs crossed at both the thigh and ankles. Her arms were crossed, too, and her long chunky cardigan was at least a couple sizes too large. Lewis was working so hard, telling animated stories and chuckling at his own jokes. The woman was as quiet as she was cold and thin.

Wren watched Lewis and the woman, peripherally unpacking the extent of their relationship. Definitely a first date, and judging from their mutual stiltedness, they were at the nascent stage of online dating wherein each party must determine which assumptions gleaned from the other's online persona actually hold in real life and which do not reconcile with the reality of the person before them.

Lewis wore a marigold yellow shirt that matched the adjacent flower beds.

Wren told herself not to stare. *Do not stare,* she told herself. *You are here to eat salad and read.*

Yet eavesdropping on Yellow Shirt Guy was much more entertaining than reading about big data.

"Just moved back from New York," he said.

". . . used to live in Denton before I quit music school. Now I teach yoga," she said.

"You're a yoga instructor? That's super cool," he replied.

Yellow Shirt Guy vaulted another joke, and when Bony Legs Girl didn't laugh, Wren made bold and deliberate eye contact with him and smiled.

Do not stare, Lewis told himself. *You are on a date with Bony Legs Girl, not Salad Girl.*

*   *   *

Lewis walked his date to her car, giving her a loose hug with as little of their bodies touching as possible when it was time to say goodbye.

Afterward, when he was sure she had driven away, Lewis sprinted back to the café. He didn't want Salad Girl to leave before he introduced himself; he had a feeling about her.

Yellow Shirt Guy stood above Wren seconds later, panting but trying to appear nonchalant.

"I'm glad I didn't miss you," he said.

"Hi."

"I was hoping I could get your number?"

"Not wasting time," Wren replied.

"Nope."

"Weren't you—fifteen minutes ago—here on a date with another girl?"

"That was nothing. A friend. What is your name?"

"Wren."

"Wren. Like the bird?"

"Yes."

"Wren," he repeated. "I'm Lewis."

"Lewis," Wren said, deliberately letting the letter S at the end of his name drag for a second longer than she normally would. "Did you know your shirt matches the flower beds?"

"Thank you. I mean— No, I didn't."

A few more lines of small talk became a four hour conversation, the large table between them seeming smaller and smaller as time passed. They got up only because the employees began stacking chairs and sweeping beneath tables.

Before they said goodbye, Lewis wanted to kiss her but hesitated, and in the pause, Wren handed him her business card.

Lewis did not even wait to get home to look her up. He sat in his Honda Accord with the business card on his knee and Google open on his phone, jittery with the upstarts of new infatuation, trying to learn everything he could about this woman whose name was Wren. Wren, like the bird. *Wren*.

When Lewis learned she worked in finance, his high hopes began to fade. Lewis wondered if she would have given him her number if she'd known he was a high school theater teacher.

He imagined the men Wren usually dated. Were they the adult prototypes of the fraternity brothers and business majors Lewis made fun of (and secretly envied) in college? The ones who did not have class on Friday, drove seventy-thousand-dollar sports cars, and partied with their parents' money in Cabo for spring break? In college, Lewis was critical of these confident future millionaires because he was jealous. And he was jealous because he was insecure. Maybe he was still.

But you have your art, Lewis told himself when he was still thinking of Wren four days later. *You can't offer her riches, but you are more interesting than any of those guys. You lived in New York!*

Then Lewis legitimately laughed out loud at himself and thanked god he had not said that aloud to anyone.

At last, Lewis composed a text:

Hi it's me, Lewis Woodard, guy in the yellow shirt. I've been thinking about you, and I apologize for not reaching out sooner. Would you like to grab a beer this weekend?

After he sent it, three gray bubbles appeared immediately, and then Wren's message:

Yes.

"Why did you move back to Texas?" Wren asked early in their first date, sitting by his side at a picnic table in the yard behind a brewery.

Lewis had left New York City for so many reasons, but because this was a first date, he decided to share only one.

"I think I missed the sky. Maybe the buildings and concrete started to take a toll on me. It felt hard to breathe." Lewis instantly regretted sharing something so opaque with this practical and accomplished woman. "That probably sounds weird."

"No," Wren replied, leaning toward him with a hand cupped beneath her chin. "That's not weird at all."

After a year together, Lewis thought he could tell when Wren was thinking about her mother; her forehead would crinkle, and her gaze would drift to the floor.

Wren's countenance held this very expression during a surprise hot-air-balloon ride over Lake Travis, the culminating event of her birthday weekend. Lewis decided to take a risk.

"What do you miss about her?" he asked, hoping he was reading her mind accurately.

As they floated over the lakeside mansions during a Creamsicle sunset, Wren told Lewis how her mother could identify every bird by name, bake bread from scratch, and grow a garden in an eggshell. How, since the loss, Wren looked at her hands first thing every morning and pretended they were her mother's hands—hands that never left her, hands that lived on in the foggy transition between sleeping and waking.

"So, everything?"

Wren nodded.

"Yeah," she whispered, her eyes suddenly glassy. "Everything."

Wren, age nine

School came easily to Wren because she enjoyed knowing how things fit together. She also had an extraordinary ability to memorize anything quickly. She spotted her teachers' mistakes and inconsistencies but was reprimanded for remarking upon them, so Wren became the quietest girl in class.

When Wren finished her assignments before her peers, the teachers allowed her to read a library book until the other students completed theirs. In books she could experience different realities and learn from the people in them. In books, Wren saw how people made mistakes. She decided she would not be one of them. Somehow, some way, she would grow up to be perfect.

At Wren's fourth-grade parent-teacher conference, Wren's teacher told her mother, Angela, that Wren was an exceptional student, but she was isolated socially, preferring to read at recess next to the teacher rather than engage with her classmates. This was no surprise to Angela. Wren had been quiet and observant since she was a baby. Still, Angela wanted to do everything she could to help her daughter, and if the teacher thought Wren's introversion was a problem, Angela would take it seriously.

Angela decided to make Wren's tenth birthday a real event. At first Wren was reluctant, but the more Angela talked about the possibilities, the more Wren got excited. Angela reserved a pavilion at the park. Two Saturdays before the party, Wren and Angela made twenty-six invitations by hand on multicolored construction paper with the date, time, and place. Wren hand-delivered each invitation to her classmates' cubbies on Monday.

The morning of Wren's birthday party, February 27, Angela gave her a haircut in the backyard. Afterward, they frosted cupcakes, painted each other's nails bright pink, and made Wren a paper crown.

It was a gift of a day, 75 degrees and sunny, the kind of seasonal anomaly that usually preceded a week of ice and snow.

"How lucky. What a perfect day for a party," Angela said.

"What a perfect day for a party," Wren parroted, giddy.

They got to the pavilion an hour early to set up before the party. Angela hung streamers while Wren arranged twenty-six bingo cards on the tables. But at one o'clock, the start of the party, no one had arrived.

"People are probably just running late," Angela said, hoping she was right.

Finally, at half past one, a car drove slowly toward the pavilion, but when it got close, Wren saw a small head slink down in the passenger seat. Then the car drove away.

"That was someone from my class," Wren said.

"I bet something came up. I'm sure others are on their way!" Angela replied.

At two o'clock, Angela did not want to say the painful, obvious thing aloud. So she put all twelve candles on a dozen cupcakes and had Wren stand on a bench while she serenaded her with a very enthusiastic rendition of "Happy Birthday." Wren burst into tears before the end of the song, sobbing so hard she had to gasp for breath. The crown they'd made together fell off Wren's head and into a puddle.

"Nobody likes me. Nobody even knows I exist. I hate myself."

Angela took Wren's hands, but Wren pulled away and plopped down on the bench.

"Well, *I* love you. You are the best person I've ever met, my favorite human on this planet."

Dutifully, Wren blew out the candles.

As they gathered bingo cards and streamers, Angela became quietly furious at these kids she did not know and their parents' punishing judgment. Angela was also angry at herself. This was her fault, too, for being the wrong kind of mother. The kind of mother who got pregnant at fifteen without a husband.

"You know," Angela said as she started the truck, "maybe this is all my fault. On the invitations, I forgot to write *RSVP.*"

"It's okay, Mom. I didn't really want a party anyway."

For the next two days, Angela and Wren ate cupcakes for dinner. It was fun at first, but by the second dinner, they both admitted they were utterly sick of sweets.

B efore Lewis, Wren hadn't been in a relationship since her early twenties. Before Lewis, her relationships were transactional, brief, and uncommitted. Few lasted longer than a first or second date.

But Lewis changed everything and all of her. She hated the cliché, but Lewis gave her something she didn't even know she needed. Wren needed it so much she could not resist him once he found her, but when she began to love him, Wren battled indecision and fear, the convincing voice telling her that loving was a risk she could not afford.

During their engagement, Wren revealed after a venue tour that she thought weddings were a total racket and marriage was nothing more than a government document existing for tax and legal benefits.

"I'm not sure what you're saying." Lewis balked in the Dallas Arboretum parking lot.

"I'm saying I don't feel social pressure to spend thousands of dollars on a venue. A wedding is a meaningless social performance."

Lewis understood what she meant, but he was sad. Lewis saw weddings in a very different way. He loved how it was a performance; a performance based on real love seemed like the very best thing. He was, after all, an actor.

While Lewis was occupied hiding his diagnosis from her, Wren became similarly distraught with a private issue. She realized she was wrong about weddings. Their wedding must have had meaning, because ever since the ceremony, something had changed within her. She could not sleep.

By the time they were engaged, Wren thought she had vanquished her fear of love and commitment. She had never felt so free and happy. But marriage awakened a new and unexplainable anxiety. During the day, Wren could manage it through suppression, but at night, the beast overpowered her. It wasn't Lewis as a person, the depth of her love, or the fact of their commitment that disturbed her. It was that she knew how easily they could fail each other.

When she couldn't bear being still and alone with herself any longer, Wren would slip out of bed and walk in the neighborhood until the sun began to glow behind the rooftops.

Beyond the spheres of light cast by streetlamps, Wren saw raccoons, opossums, skunks, and stray cats. Once, she saw a fox prowling across front lawns. Twice, a coyote bolted the moment it saw her. After these sightings, Wren caught her mind wandering, wondering what it would be like to be an animal with such uncomplicated, reasonable fears.

Wren was better with meal planning and financial matters. Lewis was better with obscure pop culture references and spontaneous art projects involving, for example, neon-colored spray paint, a jigsaw, and the entire garage. Some days they balanced each other nicely. Other days Wren and Lewis existed on opposite ends of the house, not speaking.

Lewis had a dream to one day live in a treehouse. In premarital counseling, Lewis even named "treehouse living" as one of his serious life goals.

He drew informal treehouses as well as epic trees to support his hypothetical houses—redwoods, sequoias, and banyans, trees that would never grow in Texas. But most of Lewis's trees were imagined and did not exist in nature at all, with their corkscrew trunks, umbrella-sized leaves, and hammock-shaped branches.

After they moved in together, Wren found treehouse drawings all over the house, on scrap paper, bills, invitations, receipts, old cardboard boxes, and junk mail. Lewis's ideas came with the immediacy of lightning, and he left each drawing in the exact place the idea came to him.

Wren loved Lewis's ideas but had little patience for their accompanying clutter.

"Can I throw this away?" Wren would ask, holding up a drawing, and Lewis would answer her very seriously.

"No. We need to save that."

"What about this one?"

"Save that one, too."

"Lewis, this is a Taco Bell napkin. Are you sure you don't want to transfer your sketch to something sturdier?"

"I want to keep it like it is."

Wren bought him a plastic file with three dividers and explained how he could store, and even organize, his drawings in the compartments. Lewis appreciated organization as a concept but never remembered to practice it.

In the end, it was still Wren finding drawings under sofa cushions, on the bedroom floor, beneath dirty coffee mugs, and between pages of books. Wren, dutifully organizing the drawings for him.

On the third anniversary of their first date, Lewis set up an elaborate picnic beneath the E-Z UP they bought for an OU–Texas tailgate. When Wren got home, sweaty from a spin class, and saw this display from the kitchen window, she was almost certain Lewis was about to propose. They had talked about it, even purchased the ring together, but Lewis said he still wanted to surprise her with the timing.

"Hey, Wren!" Lewis called to her, even though she could not hear him through the glass.

For two years, Wren inwardly grimaced when people asked if she and Lewis planned to get married. The fact that she was a woman of childbearing age in a relationship with a man was suddenly a topic that strangers, acquaintances, family, and friends felt it was their right to probe and discuss.

Men don't get asked these questions! Wren would thunder to Lewis after a dinner party or work event. *Next time, I'm telling them that our relationship is none of their business! I'll say that we want to live in sin until the goddamned day we die!* Lewis was on the same page; he only wished people would ask him the questions instead of Wren, to save her from getting so upset.

Wren actually tried telling people flat out that her marital status was not their concern, but it did not stop the same people from asking her again a few months later with renewed and entitled necessity, as if the answer would change their own life in some marked way, *When are y'all thinking of getting married?*

Nearing age thirty-five, she finally realized the questions would never end but rather, transmute and graft themselves onto different personal topics. Wren, tired of being annoyed, surrendered. Fielding officious, gendered questions was part of being a woman in the world, and the world did not care that she was an extremely private person. So, as well-meaning people pressed on with their queries, she smiled coyly, played along, and remembered that she was the leader of her own life.

Unexpectedly, a new phase swallowed her like a big wave. Wren was interested in the idea of being married. And then she really wanted it.

"What is this?" asked Wren, hoping that Lewis would not propose under an E-Z UP (of all places) when she smelled of exercise and her hair was such a disaster.

"You know those palapas on the beach? The ones you see in paradise travel pictures?"

"Palapas on the beach?"

"The straw-hut thingies. In places like Bali. Bora-Bora. Tahiti. I wanted to take you there this afternoon, but this was the best I could do," Lewis said, winking.

"Well, I've never been to Bora-Bora. It's lovely here."

"Would you like a piña colada?" Lewis said, handing her a drink he'd fashioned inside a coconut shell.

"I would love a piña colada," Wren replied, relieved that she was not yet engaged yet still practicing what Lewis had taught her about improvisation, *Yes, AND?*

Lewis was an actor first but always believed he had it in him to write one great play. In fact, it was one of the earliest things Wren learned about him, but she soon realized that Lewis's desire to talk about playwriting was greater than his desire to actually do it.

He came up with many interesting storylines, and historically, they all went nowhere. Wren encouraged him to write. Lewis encouraged himself to write. But it was never the right time to write. And yet Lewis could not let the dream die.

"What if it's a play about a couple . . ."

"Uh-huh."

"A lesbian couple."

"Go on."

"And they wanted to have a baby."

"Huh."

"But they can't decide which one of them will carry the child. So they decide to be pregnant at the same time."

"Okay."

"The doctors impregnate each woman with the other woman's brother. Or maybe its cousins. I haven't decided yet."

"Complicated."

"After they're inseminated, the doctor says something that makes the women paranoid that the samples got mixed up. The rest of the play follows their pregnancies, and because they're so obsessed, it brings up all these insecurities in their relationship, and it looks like their marriage may completely fall apart."

"Wow. And the ending?"

"I don't know yet, but I think I'll call it *Inbreds*?"

"You said that like it was a question."

"It is a question. It's the biggest question in the play."

"It sounds funny."

"Yes, funny and dark. Like, maybe we shouldn't be laughing because the stakes are so real and intense, and right when it feels like it's too much chaos to bear, there will be a moment of transcendence—a spiritual lightness somewhere near the end of the second act, just lightly hinted at, of course, nothing that hits you over the head—and after everything is in pieces, we'll wonder if the characters can repair. The end of the play will ask a real question. Like, is it ever possible to rebuild? Or, after time, is every relationship just a little bit broken?"

"Lewis, seriously, you should write this one."

"Maybe, yeah. But probably not."

"Why?"

"It's going to be a very busy semester."

And then Lewis caved, as usual, to the chatter of resistance, the recitation of his very important responsibilities, the weighty things that would require all his life force, attention, and creative energy, why he should not do the thing that was, deep down, most important to him.

To distract himself from the deepening realization that he would not be able to keep his diagnosis from Wren much longer, Lewis bought four kites, each a different color, on his way home from a summer staff meeting at the school.

"A boy was selling kites on the side of the road," Lewis explained when Wren got home from work that evening.

"Really?"

"Yeah. I got four."

"How nice. But why four?"

"One for each of our hands."

Turns out, getting four kites up between two people was trickier than Lewis imagined. They settled on flying them one at a time.

Each kite went up, up, up, until the spool was empty and the string, taut. Wren and Lewis stood at the end of the driveway, watching the kites float between their hands and the blue, so free for something bound to the earth by a string.

Lewis said the red was his favorite; Wren said she liked them all.

On Mother's Day, a few weeks after the wedding, Lewis went to brunch with his parents while Wren drove two hours to the lake in Oklahoma where she lived until she was ten. The first year they were together, Lewis wanted to go with her, but Wren declined with such surprising ferocity he did not mention it again. With this private tradition, there was no need to sit awkwardly at another mother's table with a seven-dollar greeting card, wondering what to do with her hands, what to do with her heart.

Wren dug her oar into the bottom of the lake, pushing off and coming up with a string of algae. Her canoe cut through the still water. The rhythm came right back to her. *Right, hold, left, hold, right, hold, left, left, right, right, hold . . .*

It had been eleven years.

Wren took a deep breath, closed her eyes, and asked herself what she always did at the lake: *What do I need?* She never knew the answer.

When she perspired through her shirt, Wren paddled back and smiled remembering how, when she was a girl, her mother told her canned peaches were alien brains. Wren announced this fact loudly to everyone in the school cafeteria the next day. Kids called her stupid and crazy as she tried to convince them. But Wren would not waver. She knew it was true. It had to be. Her mother told her so.

Before driving back to Dallas, Wren had a picnic by the carp feeding area next to the Bait 'N Tackle Shop. No one recognized her, not anymore, but she recognized them. They were all the same. The families with their Jet Skis and pontoon boats. The families with fathers who drank Coors and loaded the boats with water skis, ice chests, life jackets, and towels. The mothers who slathered SPF 50 on pasty blond boys who could not stand still. The families who saw only one another and not the woman on the bench who could not remember her own mother's face on Mother's Day.

The truth was, Lewis didn't first meet Wren at the café. He'd met her months before, in a daydream. Lewis never shared this with her, knowing Wren would probably perceive it as one of his metaphorical ideas rather than an experience that had actually happened to him.

The daydream occurred like this:

As Lewis stood in line at the supermarket with a bag of green apples and a package of frozen chicken, his vision glazed over, and he saw the image of a woman—Wren, he would know later—walking toward him as if they were friends who had just found each other in a crowd. Then they had the kind of conversation that was of simultaneously no and great importance:

"Hello, nice to see you," Lewis said.

"Hi, yourself," Wren replied.

"What a wonderful daydream," Lewis remarked.

"Yes. Have we met before?" she asked.

"No, I think this is the first time," he replied.

Lewis had the daydream, that odd premonition, years ago. All along, he'd kept it to himself. (Even for Lewis, it was a little bizarre.) Now his hidden diagnosis made this other buried truth seem less weighty.

"I met you in a daydream, you know," Lewis blurted out at dinner one night. "I knew you before I knew you."

"That's really sweet," Wren replied, just as Lewis had predicted. "I suppose I feel the same way."

"There is something else."

I am becoming a great white shark, Lewis thought, and backed away from the ledge. He could not say it, even though he knew he had to, he knew he should.

"Yeah?"

"I forgot. It must not have been important."

"You will remember if it is."

For different reasons, Wren and Lewis held a mutual ambivalence about having children. Lewis could not imagine himself as a father with his core dream still unfulfilled. Would he just get engulfed in the endeavor of fatherhood and lose himself, his aspirations, forever? Besides, how could he tell a child they could do anything if their own father was living proof the sentiment was not true?

Wren's uncertainty came from a desire to be the antithesis of the kind of woman who usually emerged from her hometown; the opposite of her mother, who started taking care of people before she made something of her own in the world.

Yet lately, strange thoughts had begun to creep around Wren's mind, ideas that would not leave her alone.

JUNE

After a big morning thunderstorm, summer seemed to celebrate itself. The sky was a little too blue, and the grass was a little too green, and the daylilies, sparkling with rainwater, were perfect orange. With the heat and humidity momentarily at bay, Wren and Lewis sat on the patio on their matching lounge chairs, watching the clouds fill with bright white light and absorbing the "weatherlessness" (what Lewis called these fantastic departures from the vehement heat).

Wren pretended to read; instead, arranging words in her mind: *Lewis, what do you think about us having a baby?* She predicted he would respond with either *Now?* or *Why?*

Lewis pretended to draw in his sketchbook; instead, imagining he could breathe through his feet, an old pre-audition ritual. He'd promised himself he would tell Wren about the diagnosis by the end of the weekend, and now it was Sunday afternoon. With his deadline looming, he could not focus on anything but the revealing moment that would change their lives forever. In his head, Lewis counted: *One, two, three—*

"I have something very important to tell you," Lewis said.

"Okay," Wren replied, expectantly.

Lewis looked at his hands, took a deep breath, squinted at the sun, and cleared his throat. All this preparation and rumination, and he still couldn't say it.

So he sat up, lifted his shirt, pushed down the elastic band of his boxer shorts, and let his body start the conversation. Lewis closed his eyes. He did not want to remember Wren's first reaction to the belt of white and gray sharkskin on his lower abdomen and back.

"What is that?" she asked after a long pause.

Lewis dropped his shirt and opened his eyes. "You know my nose issue?"

"Yes."

"And my dehydration?"

"What is it? You heard back from Dr. Ramirez?"

Lewis nodded.

"I did. I've been scared to tell you. I'm sorry. I've been diagnosed with a mutation. Carcharodon carcharias."

The color left Wren's face, and her heart dropped one thousand stories. "A mutation . . . carcharias? Which one is that?"

The clear day with the too blue sky, and the too green grass, and the perfect orange daylilies was no longer a pleasant place. This patio would forever be the starting place of the end.

"Great white shark."

Wren's forehead crinkled. Her gaze drifted to the concrete floor.

"They say the first year of marriage is the hardest," she said at last as she squeezed his hand.

It was the most hopeful thing anyone could have said, a bypassing of the truth, because there would not be another year to measure against this first one.

Two weeks passed. They avoided speaking of the real thing, their new future, in blunt terms, and went about their lives superficially. Small talk about domestic matters, schedules, news, and weather was easy for Wren but draining for Lewis, who found inauthenticity suffocating.

On Friday night, Wren asked, "Do you want to cook or go out?"

"What do we have in the fridge?"

"Not much. We could have breakfast for dinner."

"Yeah?"

"Avocado toast, poached eggs, a little fruit salad."

"I don't know."

"Or I could make spaghetti."

"You don't like spaghetti."

"I don't, but I'd eat it."

"Let's do the toast."

"You don't want toast."

"Toast is fine. It's just boring."

"Do you want to order takeout? Let's order takeout."

"Sure. I'll eat whatever you order."

"Maybe Thai?"

"I don't know. It's always so spicy."

"You can choose your level."

"I'm not that hungry."

"Actually, me, neither."

SCENE: The Real Thing

The night of the solstice, Wren and Lewis play game after game of Jenga on the dining room table.

    Lewis taps a block and causes the tower to tumble. After the crash, he pauses for a beat and stares blankly at the table, lost in thought.

WREN: You know the rules. Loser rebuilds.

LEWIS: Are you mad at me?

WREN: No. Why?

LEWIS: You sound mad.

WREN: Just stressed.

LEWIS: I'm sorry you're stressed.

WREN: How are you feeling?

LEWIS: The same. Itchy, thirsty, tired.

WREN: Oh.

LEWIS: We're going to live our lives, like we always have.

WREN: You keep saying that.

Lewis liked to take Wren to the symphony and sit in the front even though it was more expensive. Lewis liked to close his eyes, open his palms to the clouds, and let the music wash over him. Wren gradually adopted his practice. At first she felt a bit embarrassed, wondering what people thought of them, but soon she couldn't enjoy the music any other way. There was a fearlessness to Lewis's method, like jumping into a body of water without first testing its temperature.

After he picked up the game, Lewis chose a favorite from the last symphony they attended, Elgar's "Nimrod." He extended his arm to dance.

It was not really a dancing song but, rather, the kind of music that made you want to nestle into the arms of someone wonderful and stay there forever.

Through the music's swells, they swayed, and they knew, and they held each other, and they knew, and they melted, and they knew, and they knew, and they knew: Everything would be different and difficult soon.

When the movement was over, Wren held his ears softly framing his face with her hands.

"Tonight's a strawberry moon," Lewis said.

"We should go to bed," Wren replied. "It's late."

"A moon like this won't happen again until 2086. We'll be a hundred years old."

They were outside for most of the night, barefoot on the grass, moths tickling their ears, rocking back and forth on the hammock Lewis had insisted on including on their wedding registry.

"Well, this has got to be the boldest, brightest moon I've ever seen," Wren said.

"I've seen all kinds of moons in my life, and this is the best one," he agreed.

Lewis gazed at the moon and then to Wren and once more at the moon and back to Wren, realizing, startlingly, he could not tell the two entities apart.

In this evanescent moment, the love of his life and the moon became indistinguishable from each other, casting everything Lewis feared about the future in the real but temporary light of goodness. Time suspended, Lewis promised himself to always remember Wren like this, a masterpiece memory—hair splayed behind her, a small restful smile, cutoff shorts, and the T-shirt from last year's spring musical, *Little Shop of Horrors*.

Suddenly, a gossamer prescience too delicate to name floated before him, and then it became him. This was the place: his life's true destination, the point of work, fortitude, hope, and valor. Lewis understood everything now. And then, faster than the insight came to him, it faded, and he was once again a man with an incurable disease who loved his life, his wife.

In the same moment, awe replaced Wren's usual mental activity, trying to know, do, plan, and control. Wren was simply a human being existing on the surface of Planet Earth, and he, and he, and he—Man of Sea. It just was.

They were, at once, thirty-five and a hundred years old.

In the morning, they lied over coffee and oatmeal:

"How did you sleep?" asked Lewis.

"Like a baby. You?"

"Like a rock."

As a high school drama teacher, Lewis spent his days swiftly commanding rooms of pimply egos. He developed a surprising fondness for the transition from adolescence to adulthood. He imagined it was his young self in their seat and tried to give them good advice:

Take a shower even if you think you don't need one.

Defiance is easy, but courage is harder.

In the long run, many subjects in high school are not all that important, but you must try, for at least fifty-five minutes a day, to pretend they are.

Every August, Lewis would bemoan his crop of creatively arrested students, ranting to Wren about the crushing effects of neoliberalism in public schools and how a chronic lack of arts funding was a form of systemic social oppression. *If we don't value artists as the most visionary among us, what will be left of this world? What is left but the pursuit of more money, more things?* But by closing night of the fall play, Lewis's rants would transform into impassioned speeches about humankind's ability to work with their differences, think together, and adapt. The students learned lines and constructed worlds, but most of all, they came in as strangers and left as a collective of best friends.

Lewis began by softening his students into a new play, telling them all about the human significance of the work, its writer, and the trials they experienced while writing the play; how, in performing it, they became a part of its legacy; it was an honor, he said, to take lines, the playwright's distilled vulnerability, and make them one's own. He would say acting is paying homage to the visionaries who had the courage to go for it; acting is freeing the parts of oneself living secretly, ashamedly, in memory and regret; acting is living at the height of one's emotional possibilities; acting is crafting reality in the name of pretend; acting is the one time when no one suffers the consequences of truth.

Lewis also told them of transcendent performances he'd witnessed in New York, moments on the stage that bristled with humanity and heart when he was certain he'd been dislocated in time and sent to another world, a world where invisible energies made all words feel new and made up; he told his students they, too, could access these moments with each other; externally, people would praise their acting, their talent; but the pursuit's purpose was not for recognition or even mastery of the art form but for the discovery of danger, of the edge, of the nameless, tireless dragon breathing not fire, but hope into the experience of being human; it was their duty, he'd say, to deliver the message: Faith lived in the darkest rooms.

Lewis was the sort of educator who changed his students, especially the young men, on a formative and fundamental level. As a grown man comfortable with his own vulnerability, he inspired his students to enter an uncommon domain, a place where fear, sadness, and rage were worthwhile experiences rather than things to smile through or tuck away. Furthermore, Lewis was so occupied with the work of teaching that he did not notice how much he was admired, and this ignorance of his own greatness only garnered him more respect.

Of course, if the role of a lifetime fell from the sky, Lewis would leave teaching without a thought. His students must have sensed this priority, because they gave their best when he asked for it, perhaps knowing that for as much passion and energy as Lewis gave to teaching, there was always somewhere else he would rather be.

Now that his diagnosis was in the open, Lewis felt a renewed longing to be onstage, to leave his mark, to return to New York. He hadn't felt it this intensely since he was a nineteen-year-old psychology major at the University of Texas, hanging around the theater department so often the faculty thought he was in the program. Back then Lewis was counting the days until he could leave Texas forever and move to New York City.

A college education was a formality to appease his parents, who would not pay for him to study something financially impractical, like acting. When Lewis graduated at twenty-two, he told his parents he no longer wanted to go to graduate school (like that was ever his plan), sold his car, and moved to the city.

After two years in New York, Lewis realized he would need to prove his ability in a different way than he'd expected. He learned that only a small part of success as an actor had to do with being talented and right for a role. Hundreds of actors were talented and right.

To rise above the masses, Lewis tried to execute every known strategy. He needed to take expensive acting classes with influential, connected acting teachers. He needed to court up-and-coming playwrights. He needed to pay to perform for casting directors in showcases. He needed to mail hundreds of postcards with his résumé and picture on them to every talent agent in the city. He needed an extraordinary headshot to communicate the totality of his unique essence, a photograph that would stand out among the other thousand pictures of actors who looked just like him. When all else failed, he needed to prove himself as a multitalented Renaissance man; he needed to raise money to write, direct, produce, and act in his own work; all of this so the industry would be thirsty to work with him.

As a teenager, he thought *sticking with it* as an actor referred to the grind of auditioning. By twenty-three, Lewis knew getting a legitimate theater audition was almost as uncommon as landing a part. Sticking with it meant surviving in New York.

Lewis critiqued the young actors he knew who'd found success early, after one or two years in the city. He secretly hoped those actors with easy and early success would fail and be exposed for their averageness. And when they faltered, it would be his time. His time to step into the light, center stage, seasoned and prepared.

This critical lens sustained Lewis for a very long time, but it also made him bitter. In his lowest moments, Lewis wondered if he might be the average one after all. At times he felt he would rather die than find out the truth.

By the time Lewis was twenty-nine, he no longer felt special or divinely chosen for the actor's life. He no longer looked down his nose at college friends who became dentists, lawyers, accountants, or fathers of two. He no longer thought his dream, acting on Broadway, was possible.

Why do I still want to do this? Why do I need acting? Lewis asked himself, often.

He could recite his old answers, but they no longer held the same potency. He wanted to be an actor because he loved to transform. He could do things onstage he could not do in real life. He could fight his enemy or land a joke. He could fall in love with a narcissist, man, or goddess. He could die for the revolution. The stage also was a wonderful place to grapple with life's ambiguity, and because there was an audience, Lewis felt seen. Even loved. But an audience's love was not the kind that would go home with him and eat dinner. It was love at a distance, and Lewis wanted to be held and touched. By another human. By real life. *Could it be that I am lonely, and the theater was never meant to be enough?*

Lewis also felt a new and surprising longing for Texas.

He missed driving and parking lots. He missed big skies and the prairie. He missed small talk and people who took their time. He missed January weeks with all 70-degree days and the football hype in the fall. He missed his parents.

On Lewis's thirtieth birthday in late March, it snowed nine inches, and he spent the day in the West Village, walking designer dogs, belonging to other people. As he scooped countless mounds of dog poop, he realized life did not have to be so hard. And then a second thing occurred to him, not as a backup plan but as a truly excellent idea:

I could move back home to Texas! I could teach!

Yes, he could find personal significance by helping others find theirs. He could give people the comfortable space to try, and if Lewis was an expert in anything, it was trying.

Lewis was thirty-two and had been teaching for a little over a year when he met Wren, just when the new gig had begun to lose its shine. Working with students was fulfilling, but staff meetings, creating and grading assignments, and interacting with stage parents was exhausting and tedious.

Lewis wrestled with the part of him that still wanted to be an actor. He wondered if he was truly done with New York. Had he cut his time too short? When Lewis got depressed about what he was missing, Wren drew out the possibilities:

"Start auditioning again. You say all the time that there are Equity theaters right here in Dallas doing great and interesting work."

"I spend all day teaching and every evening in rehearsal with my students. I just don't have the time."

"Well, you could quit. Let's move to New York or Los Angeles. You can try out for plays and TV again. I can support us while you get started."

"It is appropriate and, some might say, poetic to fail in one's twenties, but I would be humiliated if I failed at the same thing in my thirties, especially when you are sacrificing, too."

"It wouldn't be a sacrifice."

Wren's encouragement both calmed and frightened Lewis. He wished it were Wren who was holding him back.

But now, four years later, there was something bigger than fear keeping him from a career on the stage. Lewis's vision was changing dramatically.

Colors were quickly losing their vibrancy. Wren's bright red nail polish dulled to maroon. His sky blue sedan to cobalt. Their daisy yellow stand mixer next to the refrigerator, a dull blond. Lewis knew what was coming. Eventually, his world would be Dorothy's Kansas before Oz, a world in black, gray, and white.

Reflexively, Lewis dreamed of New York as both a comfort and a distraction from reality. But unlike the visions of his youth, Lewis did not imagine the city as a fantasy he had not yet experienced. Now he imagined New York exactly as he'd left it, with all its light, movement, and noise.

Most of all, Lewis imagined the colors. White-pink cherry blossoms. Pride flags. Flashing red and gold marquees. Central Park's emerald lawn. Mustard yellow taxicabs. Deep red strawberries in bodega windows. Rainbow confetti, shimmering in the air and then swirling and saturated in oily puddles on the street. All those years, while he was so focused on one thing, being an actor, he took for granted all that was already his. All the colors to see.

Lewis and Wren invited his parents over for Sunday dinner to broach the news of Lewis's diagnosis.

On the day, Lewis and Wren prepared an elegant but solemn dinner for four and rehearsed the conversation.

Lewis would break their hearts after dessert, chamomile tea cake with strawberry icing—his mother's favorite.

SCENE: Such Wonderful Parents

Lewis and Wren sit across from Lewis's parents, Greg and Annie, on the sofa. For a few seconds, no one speaks.

GREG: I'm looking forward to whatever it is you want to tell us!

ANNIE: Oh, me, too.

LEWIS: Yes. Well, I do wish it were better news... I can't guarantee I'll be in good shape for Italy next summer. I've just been diagnosed with a Carcharodon carcharias mutation.

. . .

GREG: A what?

LEWIS: Carcharodon carcharias mutation.

ANNIE: What are you saying, honey? I thought you were going to tell us you were having a baby. You would be such wonderful parents.

GREG: Is that one of those animal dementias? We don't have any history of it in the family.

ANNIE: None at all.

LEWIS: We do now.

ANNIE: Oh Mylanta. Oh Mylanta.

Lewis's father rises, puts a hand on his son's shoulder, and squeezes hard. This is the closest the two men have ever come to embracing.

GREG: Do you need money?

WREN: Thank you, Greg, but we're all right.

ANNIE: How do you feel, sweetie?

LEWIS: I'm fine, I'm fine.

ANNIE: Are you smoking cigarettes again?

LEWIS: No—and good grief, Mother, that was only once, and I was fourteen.

Greg, helpless, turns on the television and tries to find something, anything, that has to do with sports.

ANNIE: Greg. No television. Not now.

Greg doesn't turn it off, but he mutes the volume and stares into the television, transfixed.

ANNIE: How long do you have?

LEWIS: Maybe ten months. A year at most.

ANNIE: Lord Jesus.

Annie begins to hyperventilate.

LEWIS: Mom, Mom, Mom. You have to breathe.

ANNIE: *I can't.*

Lewis holds his mother, and as he does, she melts into his arms, weeping.

ANNIE: Pray Jesus. Take care of my baby. Take care. Of my baby.

Wren leaves and enters again with a glass of water for Annie, who takes a sip and puts it down on the coffee table. Greg remains focused on the television.

LEWIS: We don't know about the future.
But we have each other.
And this moment, right now.

ANNIE: I hate this moment right now.

Greg snaps out of his trance and looks to Wren.

GREG: What animal is . . . Car-charo-don car . . . ?

WREN: Carcharodon carcharias.

LEWIS: Great white shark.

A hush befalls the room.

Annie steps back and puts a hand on the wall for support, anticipating that she might just fall over.

Greg closes his eyes and lowers his head in his palms.

Lewis pretends this is a play, and he is an actor who will go home to real life at the end of the night.

Wren imagines herself on the StairMaster at the gym, taking one even step after the other while never getting any higher.

Brief tableau.

Lewis had taken procrastination to its limit. Later was no longer a dependable place. He did not have decades to make theater worth remembering, to birth a reality that people would cherish in times beyond him. The best he had to offer anything was right now. And maybe that had always been true.

Thursday, June 30, 2016, was an ordinary day for most of the world, but in the life of Lewis Woodard, it was one of the most important ones. Mortality made him a realist. Mortality focused his priorities. His human body was leaving him. Yes, he would never act again, but he still had his mind. He could write something. No—he *would*.

Now, when Lewis woke uncomfortable in the middle of the night, needing water or more medication, his first thought was not of existential grief or strife but of possibility.

He didn't need New York. He would make it on his own terms. Lewis still had time to be a Great.

JULY

Lewis was determined to go to the neighborhood's July Fourth BBQ, the epic annual block party with a band, multiple smokers, a pie-eating contest, and an elaborate firework show after sundown.

Wren asked him twice if he was up to going. (She thought Lewis looked terrible but did not say so.)

Both times Lewis said he was "doing great." (He felt truly and entirely awful but did not want Wren to know.)

At the party, Lewis excused himself a few times an hour to either slather more ointment on his lower back and feet in the bathroom or refill his Solo cup with tap water to meet the demands of his relentless thirst. Fortunately, with all the commotion from sugar-loaded, screaming kids, no one flagged Lewis's behavior as unusual.

Wren spent the day trapped in draining dialogues with chatty women, pretending to be interested in things like backsplashes and Bernedoodles.

They found each other around five o'clock. Lewis gave a single firm nod that meant: *Let's just go.* Wren reciprocated. They left quietly without saying goodbye.

Wren and Lewis saw some of the fireworks from their patio. Lewis went to bed before ten. Wren stayed up cleaning; her mind would not let her sleep even though she was physically exhausted. Finally, Wren found sleep but was soon awakened by the back door closing. Lewis's side of the bed was empty but still warm.

She found Lewis stretched out on the hammock in the backyard wearing only his boxer shorts.

"What are you doing out here?" Wren inquired from the patio.

"What are *you* doing out here?" Lewis replied.

For a beat, they looked at each other as if this were a serious question deserving a serious answer, and then they burst into laughter.

"No, but really. Why are you outside?" Wren asked.

"Couldn't sleep."

"Come back to bed. I won't sleep well knowing you're out here."

"Let's sleep outside tonight. It's nice."

"On the hammock?"

"Why not."

"It's almost one o'clock."

"Who cares what time it is."

"Is there enough room?"

Lewis patted the space next to him.

"Well. All right," Wren replied and climbed into the hammock, almost tipping him out of it.

"I started writing a play," Lewis announced when they were both comfortable, lying head to toe. "I'm not just thinking and talking about it this time. I won't stop until it's done."

"*Inbreds?*"

"God, no. Not that idea. That was ridiculous. This is something different. It's a contemporary play with mythical undertones. I want it to have the kind of wise humanity that only time and hardship earn. I hope that anyone who reads it will feel immediately connected to the version of themselves that is most alive, ready, and strong."

"What's it about?"

"It's a love story about forging ahead while facing great and immediate change."

. . .

"Is it about you and me?"

"What's happened so far."

A few minutes passed, the hammock cradling them into each other like blobs of soft clay molding to each other.

After so much hesitation about sleeping outdoors, Wren was the one to drift off first. Lewis became transfixed by the rhythmic rise and fall of her chest. Wren was predictable and systematic, like a machine, even when she slept. Would this experience, his mutation, reconfigure Wren, too? What would she be like after he was gone?

Lewis tried to push those thoughts aside.

For now he only wanted more of what made her. He wanted to be crowded in, cornered, and consumed. He also wanted to give her permission, in time, to be happy. Yet permission was a strange concept in the simple framework of their relationship. Wren was of her own mind, and so was he.

So, this idea of permission, giving his blessing. Lewis wanted Wren to be happy one day; happy without him; happy with Someone Else; Someone gentle, kind, intelligent, and fun; Someone who loved her as much as he did, maybe in ways he never could, if that's what she wanted, needed, to be happy.

This thought alone was his most painful symptom so far, but the same thought was also the defining marker of what made their love true.

I can't look at everything hard enough, Lewis whispered into the stars again and again. The combination of words belonged to a character he would never play, but in that moment, he felt that the line had been written for him.

Every Wednesday morning, Lewis had consecutive appointments with a neuropathologist, a psychiatrist, and an internist in a gated, U-shaped institutional complex twenty minutes west of Denton. Lewis's appointments were always in the middle building, OCEAN 1, the center for early-stage oceanic mutations.

If the appointments brought better news, the doctors saying he was stable since the previous week, Lewis and Wren stopped for lunch at Whataburger on the way home. Yet most of the appointments, regardless of the prognosis, left neither of them feeling particularly hungry.

The complex also hosted support groups corresponding with appointment times for caretakers. Lewis said he felt comfortable doing the rounds by himself, and he encouraged Wren to try a meeting.

"You might make a friend," Lewis said after Wren showed their IDs at the gate.

"Maybe," Wren replied doubtfully. She wasn't in the mood for new friends.

Wren sat in the car for the first twenty minutes of the meeting and slipped in late so she would not have to introduce herself.

"...but in some way, I think we all resent him for it. Especially the boys," said a pink-haired woman to the group, sitting in a circle. "You know, I've seen pictures of zebras all my life and never imagined—I always thought they were such beautiful creatures."

The room murmured and nodded in support. The facilitator, a woman wearing layers of long beaded necklaces, stood up and rested her hand on the woman's shoulder.

After the meeting, Wren tried to exit without talking to anyone, but the facilitator stopped her before she could leave.

"You can't go yet! I didn't get a chance to say hello."

"Hello," Wren replied with a foot behind her.

"What brings you here today?"

"My husband is here for some appointments. Ocean 1. Carcharodon carcharias."

The facilitator's trained, compassionate gaze twitched, revealing a flicker of unmasked stigma.

"Great white shark mutations are especially dangerous for caretakers," she said gravely, as if Wren did not know.

"Yes."

"And what is your name?"

"Wren."

"Wren?"

"Yes. Wren. Like the bird."

"I hope to see you again soon."

"Sure," Wren replied, knowing she wouldn't.

Lewis's appointments went very well that day. The psychiatrist said he exhibited no signs of a mood disorder, which was quite unusual at his stage. Lewis's bone scans had not changed in three weeks, and his body temperature was as human as ever, 98.6 degrees. His only instruction was to continue eating lots of protein. This was definitely a Whataburger day.

"I forgot to ask. How was the group?" Lewis asked, unwrapping his second Triple Meat Whataburger with extra bacon.

"A woman with a zebra brother talked the entire time. I don't want to go back."

"That's too bad."

"It's okay. I'm glad I tried it."

"At least we have good doctors. At least we live near a center. At least this is not a medical mystery, like it was sixty years ago. At least we have a plan."

"Do we have a plan?" Wren instantly regretted sounding so confrontational.

"I'm trying to be positive. I'm doing all I can."

"I know. I know you are. I'm sorry, Lewis. I didn't mean it that way."

They both knew there was no plan. Not really. Lewis's mutation was like the weather; they could prepare, but they could not control a thing. Lewis and Wren didn't talk much during the drive home, and the day's bright energy faded back to its default gloomy state.

Wren climbed the gym's StairMaster for almost an hour the next morning. At this point of semi-exhaustion in her Sisyphean ascents, she usually found a breath of mental relief from the hum of everyday stress, but more often lately, she completed her workout feeling the same, if not worse, than before she started. When Wren was alone with her body, she also had to be alone with her repetitive, bleak thoughts.

Later in the locker room, Wren watched a woman put baby powder in a swim cap and tuck her straight black hair inside it. The woman was petite and barely pregnant, humming in a tone that was surprisingly husky for her flutelike frame.

From the one-way window in the locker room door, Wren watched the Tiny Pregnant Woman's unhesitating, seamless transition between walking and swimming. The other swimmers looked awkward and flailing in comparison.

When the Tiny Pregnant Woman churned the water, her hands were like spoons turning heavy cream to whipped cream to butter, stroking down the pool and back and down the pool and back and down and back and down and back and down and back. Her body, controlled by her mind, the machine; her body, lightning in the water.

As Wren prepared dinner, a two-pound bag of shrimp for Lewis and a kale Caesar salad for herself, she could not stop thinking about the Tiny Pregnant Woman.

Lewis told Wren all he wanted was to enjoy their time together, as they always had. But Wren did not know how to enjoy anything, only perfect it.

Wren always thought swimming was too gentle, quiet, and removed from the world, but the Tiny Pregnant Woman demonstrated how a woman's body could be cutting and powerful in the water.

Wren did not commit to anything lightly.

She decided to swim so much that she, like Lewis, like the Tiny Pregnant Woman, would transform into something equipped for the water. With her own mind and muscle, she, too, could engage the ever illusory margin between human and animal.

A round the time Wren decided to start swimming, Lewis purchased a
stack of books about marine life and sharks, digestible, entertaining
books with glossy pictures written for children and fans of Shark Week.
When Lewis bought the books, researching his future life in this way
seemed like a great idea, but now he was not as sure.

"If you want, I could read them, too. We could discuss things," Wren
offered.

"I'll read alone for now," Lewis replied, knowing the only thing more
terrifying than seeing his future through his own eyes would be seeing it
through hers.

Each evening after dinner, Lewis retreated to his reading chair with the new books. Reading initially proved to be a harrowing experience. So Lewis pretended he was doing character research, preparing for a new role, to trick his mind and make the work less distressing.

Through this method, Lewis's horror reverted to fascination. There were things in the books that the doctors weren't telling him. The doctors focused on subtraction, what was being taken from his human experience, but they failed to see the incredible features and traits being added in the process.

Lewis learned that he would grow to be over ten feet long and weigh at least a thousand pounds. He would be able to swim as fast as thirty miles per hour. He might also be inclined to migrate, traveling hundreds, if not thousands, of miles in a single year. But what excited Lewis most was the development of his great white shark electroreception, a shark's ability to perceive the subtle electrical fields emitted by living things for the purpose of finding prey.

This knowledge inspired an exciting idea.

With electroreception, Lewis hoped to sense her, know her, and love her even thousands of miles away in the ocean. Nothing he read indicated that electroception extended further than a couple yards. *But maybe*, he thought, *maybe if I practiced, I would never really have to say goodbye.*

When Lewis finally came to bed, he took sleeping Wren's hand in his and closed his eyes, seeing if he could sense her electrical field.

"What . . . What are you doing?" she asked groggily.

"Just seeing what it's like to love you when I can't see you."

Lewis practiced the anatomical words as if he were studying a new dialect: dermal denticles, caudal peduncle, heterocercal, ceratotrichia, chondro-cranium, ampullae of Lorenzi.

He stared into the void of the unlit living room and wondered if that was how the ocean would feel: still, dark, and cool.

Lewis also endeavored to grasp the immensity of his quiet days ahead; he wondered how and if he should prepare for the solitude. For perhaps the thousandth time in his life, Lewis had the idea to start meditating, but then he decided the timing was foolish. Meditation would be a better project for later, in the ocean, when he had nothing to do.

After two weeks of evening research, Lewis realized *it* was happening: the holiest of creative experiences, when two ingredients, the actor and character, combined to form a new substance entirely, one resembling nothing of its parent components. Lewis would enter the uncomplicated consciousness of a great white shark in extended flashes, desiring nothing but food and survival, and then return to himself, the human, with all his hopes, loves, dreams, and memories. The sensation of shifting between identities both thrilled and terrified him.

What would happen to his self in the moment of complete metamorphosis? When Lewis, the actor, became a great white shark, the character, permanently? Was Lewis's disease an art form? No, not art. Art seemed too calculated and charted. This metamorphosis was bigger and more unpredictable than art. It was a thing beyond—maybe, maybe, maybe *magic*?

Lewis scrabbled through the drawers in the coffee table for a pen so he could capture this new, electric thought:

I've had it wrong all along.
If magic exists in a real way,
it is not here to dazzle us
with all that is unreal to the naked eye.
What if magic is just mislabeled peace?
A peace that says suffering doesn't have a purpose or reason.
A peace that says meaning is the medicine.
A peace that says I don't need to know how or why.
But she'll be all right.
Wren will be okay.

During their engagement, Lewis and Wren did an online premarital coun-seling course at Wren's request, lounging on new patio furniture and enjoying the still-warm days of early fall. The section about illness and death led them to a conversation about what each would do if the other died first. They imagined the scenario of loss through the straightforward tunnel of a life well lived.

Then Lewis said he would do everything in his power to make sure they died on the exact same day. The session derailed into a comedy routine, with Lewis describing the plot of *Romeo and Juliet* as if it were his new, original story idea.

In their innocence, they failed to grasp the labor of losing a partner, how the tasks of simple existence would become logistical feats and one person's burden.

With the combined pressure of Lewis's diagnosis and the already stressful pace of her job, Wren felt herself breaking.

The men with Wren's title had stay-at-home wives who handled all the domestic labor so they could focus entirely on work and business. Wren and Lewis, however, split the housework equally, and in normal circumstances, Wren preferred life this way.

As Lewis's energy declined, Wren managed both of their lives all on her own. The burden of chores for two people, caretaking for an ill spouse, and a fifty-hour workweek was too much, even for Wren.

When life was erratic, numbers gave Wren solid ground, but lately, even her relationship with the measurable was transforming. She was making mistakes, massive numerical errors that would have cost the company hundreds of thousands of dollars had her coworkers not spotted them first.

After the first mistake, Wren corrected it and moved on, expecting herself to bounce back. After the second, she issued a professional written apology. A week later, she made her most egregious error yet. People started dropping her from meetings and email threads. Her boss, Jonathan, put time on her calendar, an hour on Friday afternoon. Wren feared the worst.

Wren worked all evening Wednesday, checking and rechecking her emails before bed.

"It's eleven o'clock. Can you please just stop?" Lewis asked. "Your phone usage is giving me anxiety."

"No. I can't," replied Wren, her voice rising.

"Are you okay?"

"Yeah. I'm fine."

"What? Tell me," Lewis demanded, sitting up taller.

. . .

"Jonathan put time on my calendar this afternoon. I've been making mistakes."

The implications of Wren's statement hung in the air. They could not maintain their lifestyle or afford Lewis's medical care, much less meet their most basic needs, on Lewis's teacher salary alone.

"Let's not worry until we know for sure. Besides, everyone makes mistakes every now and then. It is part of being human. There is no such thing as perfection."

Wren snapped:

"You're wrong, Lewis. *There is.*

My world has no space for your ambiguity.

Perfection is real, and I have to give it to them

all

the

time."

Jonathan was drinking a beer and watching ESPN with his feet on his desk when Wren entered his suite of an office.

"Can I get you a beer?"

"No, thanks, not today," she replied.

Wren, the sharp-minded powerhouse, appeared before him as a human being with tired red eyes and a wrinkled blouse.

"Have a seat. Anywhere you like."

Wren took up so little of his Herman Miller chair compared to the men who usually occupied it, leaning back, relaxed, with legs crossed in a figure four and hands laced behind their heads.

"I wanted to meet today to ask if you're doing okay," Jonathan began. "You don't have to name specifics, of course, but I want to know how we can help."

Wren, age eighteen

In high school, Wren blossomed. Her hair reached her tailbone, covering her shoulders like a curtain. She wore thrift store dresses, patched jeans, and smelled like the wind. She was kind to everyone, never fake. The girls who tried to emulate her wore the aura of having worked hard to appear effortless. The boys who asked her out had a high opinion of themselves. Wren's subsequent rise in popularity was no surprise to anyone but her.

She listened to her friends' age-appropriate plights and envied their simple lives: ruminating on the boy who made out with them under the bleachers but now ignored everything they did; trying to pass the American history test so their grades would be high enough to cheer; hiding beer from their parents; cramming seven girls into one car on Saturday night.

She did not tell anyone where she lived. She never let her friends meet her mother. No one knew Wren cleaned rooms at the Cross Timbers Motel to buy food and necessities, things her friends got easily from their parents.

Meanwhile, Wren quietly achieved. She was a National Merit Scholar. She got several full-ride scholarships to prestigious universities. She won homecoming queen and valedictorian.

Some people wanted to be more like her. Some wanted to be her. And some were not sure Wren was real. Could one person really be that great at everything? And how did she make it look so effortless?

In public, Wren wore the happy expression of a well-liked, high-achieving teenager, but beneath the charade, she was exhausted. Wren was barely surviving at home.

The morning of her high school graduation, Wren slipped out of the house in a dress borrowed from a friend and drove her mother's car, windows down, to the auditorium, practicing her valedictorian speech aloud as her hair whipped in the wind behind her.

In August, Wren embraced her mother at the Greyhound station, said goodbye, and did not look back. She was looking forward to creating a quieter identity with fewer people interested in her success. She was also relieved; in college, away from home, she could finally get some rest.

SCENE: Tiny Skin Teeth

Wren watches Lewis getting dressed from the bathroom mirror, noticing all that has changed in his physical form. His fins are more pronounced now, especially the pelvic ones jutting out above his hip bones. The beginnings of gill slits cut across his widening neck. His inhales are belabored.

Lewis meets Wren's gaze in the mirror.

LEWIS: I have an idea.

WREN: What is it?

Lewis comes to hug her from behind. He kisses her neck.

WREN: Oh. Hi.

With her eyes closed, Lewis feels the same to her as always.

LEWIS: Hi.

They start to make out.

As Wren's hands trail his body, she is careful when touching his back. He is covered in tiny toothlike scales called dermal denticles, which tend to give her a road rash–like scrape if she touches them the wrong way.

LEWIS: Hypothetically, if you were to play hooky with me today, what would the consequences be?

WREN: No. I have meetings all day.

LEWIS: Reschedule them. Everyone will be glad to have the time back. People hate meetings.

WREN: You hate meetings. I'm not a teacher who gets the entire month of July to run around town.

LEWIS: Just this once. Please. I want to go to the zoo.

WREN: The zoo?

LEWIS: Yes. The zoo.

Lewis tries to smile with his changing features, but his expression has a very different effect. His clenched, yearning face makes Wren feel guilty and then very sad.

WREN: Give me a few minutes. I'll move some things around.

At the monkey exhibit, Wren identified her favorite, and after some humorous deliberation, Lewis decided to name him Mortimer.

"Would it be so terrible if I fed him?" Lewis asked.

"The signs say no feeding."

"Other people have fed him. There's popcorn all over the place."

"The signs still say."

"Do you still have my cookie in your purse?"

"We're not feeding the monkey."

"But it's vegan. And gluten-free."

"No."

Wren tried to avoid the aquarium, but it was Lewis's idea to go inside. As they walked through the dank hallway, viewing tanks streaked with children's handprints, Lewis read each placard aloud in a cheesy announcer voice.

He paused at the sandbar shark exhibit.

"And now the crown jewel of the aquarium: the sandbar shark," Lewis said, his gusto leveled.

The shark was motionless except for the subtle swish of its tail every few seconds. The flesh near its dorsal fin was the same color and texture as Lewis's lower back. Lewis squeezed Wren's hand so hard her knuckles cracked. He released her hand to slap the tank. The shark did not move.

"What is with you today?" Wren asked, shaking her head. "Leave the animals alone."

A mother pushing toddlers in a big stroller pointed out the longnose butterfly fish. A trio of teenage girls wearing school uniforms wandered by sharing a soft pretzel. A custodian emptied the trash next to the door. When they were alone again, Lewis slapped the glass once more, even harder.

"*Stop it! Lewis!* What is wrong with you?"

Suddenly, Lewis turned and clenched Wren's shoulders as if she were the steering wheel of a race car.

"Lewis, let go of me," Wren demanded.

With a frustrated push, Lewis released Wren and began to pace the length of the shark tank.

An energy Lewis did not understand wanted to break through him. He wanted to kill a living fleshy thing. He wanted to sink his new sharp teeth into the sandbar shark, not because he was angry about any aspect of his circumstances but because he had suddenly become very, very hungry.

Lewis threw punch after punch at the glass, shouting obscenities, completely unaware of himself and his surroundings.

Wren pressed herself against the farthest wall, frightened to stay but unable to leave him alone. Three security guards stormed the aquarium, tearing Lewis away from the exhibit. After a final surge, Lewis became limp, compliant, and apologetic. The next few minutes were a blur:

Lewis was covered in his own blood.

The police came too late.

Wren explained Lewis's situation.

Security escorted them from the premises.

People craned to see the lunatics who closed the aquarium for the afternoon.

"I feel horrible. I ruined your shirt. I'll clean up all the blood in the car. God, I'm so sorry and embarrassed. I hope this doesn't make the news," Lewis lamented as Wren cleaned and bandaged his raw, bleeding knuckles in the bathroom back at home.

"I'm just glad you didn't break any bones. I shouldn't have let us go inside the aquarium."

"This is not your fault."

"Maybe next time I'll just whack you before you do something stupid."

"Are you serious?"

"Of course not!"

"Wren, today we got banned from the zoo. *The zoo*."

"Your students will eat this up."

After everything, they needed a laugh.

"I've decided to skip work tomorrow," Wren declared as she lunged for his carton of Chinese takeout that evening.

"But what about your meetings?" Lewis asked, surprised.

"Everyone hates meetings."

AUGUST

SCENE: The Stage Manager

On the first day of school, Lewis lingers in his office. He is nervous about his students seeing his new form. Meanwhile, the students, a mix of sophomores, juniors, and seniors, enter the theater classroom, talking over one another as they claim a seat in the circle of chairs. The group grows quiet as Lewis makes his presence known, passing out copies of Thornton Wilder's Our Town. *When each student has a copy, Lewis steps into the center of the circle. Their teacher/director is a very different-looking man than the one they saw in May on the last day of school.*

LEWIS: Welcome back, all.
    As you can see,
    I am not the same.
    I wasn't going to mention anything,
    but my wife thought that would be
    very strange.

The students laugh a little out of relief. Lewis still has the same essence: funny, warm, and self-assured.

LEWIS: Maybe you changed, too, over the summer.
    Speaking of summer vacation, how was it?
    Did you fall in love?

Have adventures?
Learn a new thing?
Maybe the summer was not at all what you expected.
If so, I am with you; you are not alone.
I am a very ill man
if you see mutation
as my doctors do.
But if you perceive mutation in another way,
as a *transformation,*
you might see a dramatic form with many possibilities.
I am unsure of many things,
but I am sure of this:
I want to spend my last months
as a human being
with you,
making theater
about human beings
for human beings.

Lewis scans his class and realizes half of them are near tears.

LEWIS: All right. Enough of that. We have work to do. Open your copy of *Our Town* to the first act. Decide among yourselves who reads what. A different person should read Emily and George in each act. Let's reconvene in ten minutes. Oh, and just for this read-through, I will take the part of the Stage Manager.

Lewis refused to slow down. Even though he could no longer walk without a cane, Lewis continued teaching all day and leading rehearsals for *Our Town* at night. During his rehearsals, Wren went to the pool.

Wren routinely found herself swimming in the lane adjacent to the Tiny Pregnant Woman, who had taken up evening swimming as well. The Tiny Pregnant Woman never smiled and always wore goggles with obsidian lenses and a navy one-piece swimsuit. A substantial hill now protruded from her hip bones. The Tiny Pregnant Woman swam for exactly one hour, the same as Wren. Even though they knew nothing about one another, Wren felt like she and the Tiny Pregnant Woman were already old friends, comfortable sharing silence.

As they passed each other in parallel lanes, Wren wondered who she was in her life outside the pool.

The Tiny Pregnant Woman was once a prodigy. She swam before she could talk. She competed before she could read. She decorated her bedroom with trophies and medals. Her swimming life became the family project. Her coaches said she was the best of their careers, a dream athlete, the kind of champion swimmer they all had wanted to be. Everyone said she was destined for Olympic gold. But at the trials, she failed on purpose, squandering her childhood's efforts and her family's sacrifices. She never wanted to be the best. She wanted only to be herself.

The Tiny Pregnant Woman gave up and grew up. She got a Ph.D. in chemical engineering, married a real estate mogul, and fell in love with long-distance running. She started with half marathons and progressed to hundred-mile races. She did not run to win but, rather, to lose.

Running those hundred miles alone, day and night, through the desert, the Tiny Pregnant Woman lost everything: regret, debt, religion, and ties. All that remained of her was a feral body, a body given a singular simple charge: to move, move, move, move—*move across the land as fast and far as you can.*

When it was time to start a family, the Tiny Pregnant Woman struggled to conceive.

The doctor advised her to stop running. She hated this suggestion.

Have you thought about swimming as an alternative? Many women find some gentle swimming is great exercise while trying to conceive, the doctor said. *Yes, I've thought of swimming,* she replied, containing her rising desire to punch a thing.

The Tiny Pregnant Woman thought of swimming as one would an unresolved romance. She thought of swimming one thousand times each day. She had broken its heart.

Swimming was her original sin, the lifelong sandbag on her shoulders, numbing the joy she supposed others got from moving simply through life. But most people were not born with the privilege of being elite. She had wasted it.

After a few weeks of enduring her husband's disapproving glare every time she went out for a run, she thought about trying to find joy again in the pool. She wondered if she ever had.

At first, Tiny Pregnant Woman bitterly longed to feel her sneakers pushing off the pavement on her familiar running route. She resented the hypothetical infant stealing her only peace in life. Yet, after a few laps, the pool seemed to remember her. After so long, she was home.

The more time the Tiny Pregnant Woman spent in the pool, the more the pool became like a crystal ball, revealing things about her that she could not see on her own. It seemed the pool had something to teach her about her life's purpose, and she needed to keep swimming to realize it.

When she was a girl, the pool distilled her identity to *swimmer*. Now that she was a woman, would pregnancy reduce her entire identity to *mother*?

What a tragedy it is, being a woman, she thought with relief after another negative pregnancy test. *I would rather be a million other things.*

She told her husband she wanted to stop trying. He was upset, but she was, unknowingly, already pregnant. So, that was that.

When the Tiny Pregnant Woman told her husband a few weeks later, he raised both eyebrows and cocked his head to one side, his expression of silent skepticism.

"Seriously?"

"Yeah." She felt as if she had just announced her own death.

"Wait and see," he said, matter-of-fact, returning to the article on his tablet. He knew not to get his hopes up. She had miscarried before.

"Yes," she replied. "Wait and see."

Later, they learned the pregnancy was high-risk. She was having twins. Special twins. The ultrasound did not show two tiny human hearts but, rather, the hearts of two eyases.

The Tiny Pregnant Woman thought about how the eyases would grow up to be peregrine falcons, unrelenting birds of prey. In terms of freedom, they would surpass her.

She talked to the birds in her head while she swam, trying to prepare her offspring for a life that was, as she saw it, a journey through alternating sludge and fire.

Hello.

I suppose we should know each other now.

I am your mother, a human woman.

You are my offspring, birds of prey.

This arrangement is not ideal for either of us.

So there.

We have one thing in common.

If you pierce my womb as if it is an eggshell, you will outlive me.

I am not an eggshell

but your father says

he's walking on them.

There's a saying:

"Control what you can control."

This is the butterfly stroke.

The arm movement requires full engagement of the deltoid and trapezius muscles, not to mention perfect coordination with the dolphin kick.

I could have been an Olympian.

That is the first thing to know about me.

Once Wren began swimming, she didn't care if her form looked perfect from the outside; from within, it felt so good to move.

Swimming, like numbers, contained many of Wren's favorite elements: repetition, silence, and predictability. No surprises, nothing jarring, just *down, turn, back, turn, down, turn, back; breathe, stroke, stroke, stroke, breathe, stroke, stroke, stroke, breathe* . . .

In the pool, she entered the sense memory of herself as a small girl, swimming along the back of the boat while her mother made supper. Even though Wren was still very young, few days of pure childhood remained. No one could have known she was on the brink of an adulthood determined not by physiology but, rather, circumstances.

And then, like soft rain on a hot day: the sudden relief of prophetic understanding. Wren could do for Lewis what she was too young and resourceless to do for her mother.

Plenty of smart people denied the existence of free will, but perhaps the stakes were not as high for them.

Wren had an idea—

While Lewis drafted his play after rehearsal that evening, Wren sat down with her laptop and spent a couple thousand dollars on scuba diving equipment. She usually researched something like this first, but she did not want deeper knowledge to dissuade her from what seemed to be her only good idea.

As she entered her credit card number and clicked *purchase,* her fears of failure and loss temporarily filed out of her mind, suspended above her, and took flight.

Wren, age nineteen

Wren joined a sorority with a reputation for producing powerful, acclaimed women—CEOs, senators, Nobel laureates, first ladies, entrepreneurs, writers, and movie stars. Prestige aside, the sorority house alone was a marvel to Wren.

The house was a three-storied colonial mansion with two chimneys, a U-shaped driveway, and a south-facing sunroom. The lawn was a green ocean flanked with spherical topiaries and a gazebo in the center, one of the sisters' favorite locations for group pictures, only second to the walnut staircase.

Wren shared a room with a roommate, who spent most nights with her boyfriend in his apartment off campus. A big shuttered window between their beds overlooked the neighboring sorority house's rose garden. The floor's communal bathroom opened to a row of marble sinks on one side and a massive vanity with a couple dozen velvet stools on the other. Before parties, the air would be thick with shower steam, hair spray, and perfume. To Wren, the most noteworthy feature of all was the seemingly endless supply of hot water.

Wren went out with the guys who asked her but never seriously dated anyone. She was reserved and gave the signals of someone who was very hard to get. As a result, she was attractive to every boy she met. Still, she had no interest in love and didn't understand why anyone would.

After the spring semester of her junior year, Wren stayed on campus for summer school, working part-time at the law library. The sorority house was mostly empty in the summer, and without a crowd of sisters in the kitchen, bathroom, and common areas, she could imagine clearly what it would be like to have a real home of her own one day.

For the first summer term, she enrolled in Business Statistics, and for the second, Intro to Theology to fulfill a lingering humanities requirement. Wren settled into a quiet and lovely summer routine.

In the morning, before the dew lifted from the grass, Wren jogged along the path surrounding campus. Afterward, she studied in a tufted armchair facing the big window in the common area or beneath a willow tree on the common. At eleven o'clock, she went to work at the law library, and at two, she had class. Stats came and went. Wren could not recall a time in all her life when she felt more at peace.

On the first day of Intro to Theology, the doctoral candidate teaching the course arranged the tables in a square so everyone could see one another. She corrected anyone who addressed her as professor. *Call me Rachel,* she said.

Rachel saw the world through an ironic, humorous lens. She laughed at herself, sometimes snorting, at least three times an hour, and by the end of the session, the disparate collection of students in the class felt like a gathering of old friends.

After the last class, everyone went to a bar near campus popular for its ten-dollar pitchers. A clump of students left at once, leaving a gaping hole on the bench between Wren and Rachel. Pattering nerves radiated from Wren's stomach and circulated through her body. Wren dug through her mind for any coherent phrase, language to barricade the unspoken, emergent attraction she felt toward Rachel. Then the words shot from Wren's mouth before her mind had an opportunity to consider their implications.

"You are a great teacher. I like you."

"And you are a pleasure to teach. I like you, too," Rachel replied.

Suddenly, Wren could not remember anything about anything. What was her own name? Mailing address? Date of birth? Major? Who was the president? What year was it? How in the world had she arrived at this moment in her life, one that seemed both small and inexplicably large? What did she know other than the fact that Rachel was right there? *Right there beside her.* When Rachel smiled, the corners of her lips revealed gold-capped molars. After six weeks of being eight, ten, twelve feet away from

Rachel in the classroom, Wren was now less than a foot, and everything, *everything*, was more beautiful, wonderful, and interesting up close.

"Anyway, thank you. Class was great. Fun stuff," Wren said at last. She knew her face was bright red.

Fun stuff. Wren critiqued the interaction on the walk back to the sorority house.

She tried to read but had too much energy to concentrate.

She wasn't hungry for dinner.

Wren went for her second run of the day, but she was not fatigued at all. In fact, she was the contrary—jittery and awake, soaring. What was this feeling? What could be happening? Instead of expelling this mysterious, new energy, jogging had only released more of it. Her body knew something her mind could not yet grasp. *Fun stuff.*

Later that night, Wren's laptop pinged with a new message. She scrambled out of bed to read it.

Wren,
Thanks again for your compliment today about my teaching.
I would like to know you outside of the classroom if you are open to it.
Coffee on me?
If not, I understand. No need to explain.
—R

Wren read the email four times before she understood what it meant. Could it be what she thought it was? *A date?* If this message had been from an Alpha Sig or a Beta brother, she would have offered the email to her roommate for a second opinion. But if Rachel's words meant what Wren thought they did, what she daringly hoped for, it had to be kept an absolute secret. Rachel was the most interesting thing in the universe, and Wren was smitten.

They planned to meet for coffee the next afternoon, a Friday. Wren put on every shirt she owned before settling on the first one she'd tried. On her dates with fraternity brothers, the guys picked her up, planned the dinners, and determined the pace. Wren smiled and laughed at the right cues. But eventually, she let them down gently or simply tried to disappear.

Rachel was already different. All day, Wren practiced what she would say.

Wren arrived twenty minutes early and walked around the block four times before spotting Rachel outside at a bistro table. Her hair, wrapped in a colorful scarf with a pouf of curls spilling out from the top, reminded Wren of a flower. A few tendrils fell out near her temples and looped around her ears, which had a hoop earring on one and a long beaded tassel on the other.

Wren panicked. What if she had interpreted the invitation incorrectly? What if this was only a proposal for friendship? Or, worse, mentorship?

Wren reminded herself they really didn't know each other. This whole interaction had a high chance of going terribly. She felt hot. Queasy. Tingly arms. Sweaty hands. Wren wanted to go back to the sorority house, but Rachel saw her and waved. Too late to turn around now.

"Hey there," Rachel said as Wren approached the table.

"Hi."

"How do you feel about croissants and black coffee?"

"Yeah, sound good . . ." Wren replied, trailing off and losing her words again.

Rachel smiled. "Great. I already ordered for us."

Over croissants and coffee, Rachel clarified her email, saying she wanted to get to know Wren *as a friend or something more if something more appealed* to Wren. Then she asked if Wren had ever considered a woman as a romantic possibility. Wren said that she hadn't, but the truth was, she had never really considered anyone.

When Rachel crossed her legs, she brushed Wren's calf under the table with the fabric of her long green skirt. A chill shot up Wren's spine, and her forearm hair stood on end. Wren, who analyzed everything, did not have to think one second about this.

Afternoon coffee turned into a long walk, then happy hour, dinner, and midnight. Their first day together felt like a long exhale after holding one's breath too long. They did not say goodbye until Sunday morning.

In the fall, Wren's sorority sisters expressed concern when she did not go to parties or events anymore. Wren swatted these comments away, blaming her nineteen-hour course load. She spent her secret evenings in Rachel's attic apartment, where they made elaborate dinners on lean budgets, worked in companionate silence, and lay sleepily supine in one another's arms until Wren decided it was time to make the bleary trek back to the house. Wren spent the night only when she knew her roommate was staying with her boyfriend. This way, there would be no witness to her absence, and Wren could avoid being interrogated by her romance-obsessed sorority sisters.

Rachel was over a decade older than Wren, but the age difference did not limit their connection. In fact, it was a point of speculation for each of them. Rachel wondered what would have become of her life if she'd been as driven and focused as Wren at twenty-one. Wren, on the other hand, saw Rachel as a form of predictive time travel, a way of imagining how she herself might be in her thirties.

Rachel loved to practice intricate braids with Wren's long hair—fishtails, ladders, wreaths, and twists. They took turns giving each other massages with sesame oil and read aloud instead of watching TV. Rachel talked about her research, her ideas forming like warm breath on cold glass, volleying between clarity and uncertainty. Wren listened like a child hearing a fairy tale. It did not bother Rachel that her field of study was fundamentally unknowable; that was why she chose it.

"Want to go on a road trip, have a little adventure?" Rachel asked two days before spring break as they hiked through conservation land a twenty-minute drive from campus.

"Where would we go?"

"California?"

"That's so far."

"The experience is the journey, babe."

"I don't have a lot of money right now."

"Come on," Rachel said, threading her fingers through Wren's. "We won't need much."

Wren could tell Rachel was romanticizing the trip as it happened. She even bought a Polaroid camera for the occasion. Pictures of Wren driving, sleeping, eating, and reading lined the backseat of Rachel's 4Runner. For this reason, Wren did not have the heart to tell Rachel she was having second thoughts about traveling so far by car and would prefer to turn around and spend the week at school.

"Why do you do that?" Rachel interrupted Wren midsentence, keeping her eyes on the road.

"Do what?" replied Wren.

"You change the subject every time I ask you a personal question. It's a pattern."

Rachel told stories of her childhood, college years, and twenties with such ease, but Wren never reciprocated with recollections of her own. Usually, Rachel did not pry when Wren changed the subject, but their proximity on this trip challenged Rachel's restraint.

"I don't like to talk about myself," Wren said, trying not to sound defensive even though she was.

"I feel like you don't want to be known."

"You know me."

"Do I? I think you're hiding something."

Rachel's accusation sent Wren into a spiral of anxiety.

Wren hadn't spoken to her mother since the holidays. At Christmas, she'd had to remind her mother hourly that she was not an intruder but her own daughter home from college.

The house was dirty instead of decorated, like it used to be for the holidays when Wren was young. Every corner of the house was a graveyard of dead insects. Black mold covered the bathroom walls. Her mother's bedroom reeked of dried urine, and the putrid scent permeated the house. Wren opened the windows to release some of the odor, but the wind was harsh and cold. Her mother's longtime social worker, Genevieve, delivered food every week. Cockroaches, mice, and ants pilfered the scraps her mother left on the floor.

Christmas was on a Saturday, and Wren flew back to school on Monday morning, ten days earlier than she planned. Her mother did not know the difference.

How could Wren share any of this with Rachel?

After the confrontation, Wren pretended to fall asleep in the passenger seat, but she could not quiet the intrusive voice screaming at her to run, to leave this balanced, caring woman who wanted to be her partner in life.

Passing through desert and mountain landscapes, Wren felt like a caged animal. While Rachel went on about liberation theology, Flannery O'Connor's beatific vision, and the concept of Albert Camus as a secular saint, Wren let her mind drift to the previous summer, before she met Rachel: a brief but sacred time when Wren did not have to guard the borders of her story.

SEPTEMBER

Lewis's psychiatrist always warned about the high likelihood of depression with his disease and screened him for symptoms at every appointment.

But Lewis was the opposite of depressed. He was manic—inspired, buoyant, restless, and euphoric. The experience of living in his own mind had never been so thrilling. Lewis felt like a sorcerer, overflowing with great ideas, with seemingly limitless energy to execute them.

When Lewis got home at eleven o'clock in the evening after *Our Town* rehearsals, he ate three cans of tuna, boiled a bag of frozen shrimp for continual snacking, and got to work on all his projects. First, writing the play. Second, mapping out blocking for *Our Town*. And last, working on a treehouse design for the Shumard in their backyard.

The projects came alive in him. They even collaborated with and inspired one another. For example, while he was working on the treehouse, a scene in his play would appear fully formed in his mind, and while writing the scene, Lewis would get an idea for *Our Town*. Working like this, Lewis became so absorbed he forgot he was even himself. That was, until he became hungry again.

SCENE: In the Locker Room

Wren smiles at the Tiny Pregnant Woman (TPW). TPW nods to acknowledge her, briefly making eye contact before returning her gaze to the floor.

WREN: Hi.

TPW: Hello.

WREN: Good swim?

TPW: Yes. You?

WREN: Getting there.

The women began an uncommon friendship.

SCENE: Another Day

WREN: How are you doing?

TPW: Not well. You?

WREN: About the same.

SCENE: And Another

TPW: I'm having twins. Birds.
   One of them is expressing too early.
   Wings, beak, little talons.
   Cute, right?

WREN: I'm so sorry.

TPW: Don't be. How are you today?

WREN: Good.

TPW: Don't lie.

WREN: I'm terrible.

TPW: That's fine.

WREN: Would you like to get a cup of tea?

TPW: When?

WREN: What about,
   maybe,
   right now?

TPW: I'm available now.

"I used to work for NASA. Before I got married," the Tiny Pregnant Woman said as she rolled one of her four empty sugar packets between her fingers into a dense paper ball.

"Have you been to space?"

The Tiny Pregnant Woman glared at Wren as if she had just asked a question with an obvious answer.

"No," she replied.

"What do you do now?" Wren probed.

"Research for a foundation."

"What kind of research?"

"It's complex."

"I'm asking too many questions."

"You are."

. . .

"Well, I work in finance," Wren said.

"That sounds important."

"Actually, I just took a leave of absence.

Which is why I come to the pool so much.

I need somewhere to be that's not my house.

I get tired of being stuck inside the same walls, you know?"

"Sure," replied the Tiny Pregnant Woman.

"You are a very good swimmer," Wren offered to fill the silence.

The Tiny Pregnant Woman winced. "I know."

"And—it's funny you mentioned your pregnancy the other day, because my husband has begun a Carcharodon carcharias mutation."

"That one is very rare."

"He was diagnosed right after we got married in April."

"How much time does he have?"

"A few months. Carcharodon carcharias mutations progress faster than the other mutations that begin in adulthood. No one seems to know why."

"I've read that. I'm sorry about your husband."

"I'm sorry about your twins."

"I never wanted to be a mother anyway. And now I've got two bird girls growing inside me," the Tiny Pregnant woman said without apology, staring blankly into some unseen distance.

"I never thought I'd be someone's wife. And now . . ."

Wren didn't know what was after *now,* but the Tiny Pregnant Woman understood what she meant; the future was both uncertain and difficult to imagine. During a few silent minutes, the Tiny Pregnant Woman flicked her balled-up sugar packets at the window, like a delinquent grade school kid. Wren suddenly had the intrusive impulse to ask why the Tiny Pregnant Woman had not terminated the pregnancy.

"You want to know why I haven't gotten an abortion?" the Tiny Pregnancy Woman asked.

"Well, yeah," Wren replied, feeling exposed.

"Religious reasons."

"You can't get an abortion if you're having birds?"

The Tiny Pregnant Woman felt herself on the verge of tears for the first time in years.

"The Church says angels have wings, too."

From that moment forward, Wren knew her friendship with the Tiny Pregnant Woman would be different from her others, which thrived on activities like power walking in ninety-dollar yoga pants, birthday brunching, and lamenting the cost and inconvenience of freezing one's eggs.

Wren and the Tiny Pregnant Woman shared practical, applied interests like oncoming personal devastation, terrifying sadness, and the experience of free-falling into grief and the unknown.

"I like you," Wren said as they left their table. "I think we are similar."

"Good," the Tiny Pregnant Woman replied.

After a round of Wednesday doctors' appointments, the first since Wren went on leave, Lewis fell asleep against the passenger seat window.

The appointments that day went terribly. While at first, Lewis's disease had progressed slower than expected, he was now accelerating, becoming the fastest Carcharodon carcharias mutation the doctors had ever seen. This was not a Whataburger day.

As Wren drove them home down I-35 South, she wondered what the leering drivers in the lane to their right thought when they saw Lewis pressed against the window. Did they pity them? Were they afraid?

In the last month, the top of Lewis's head had flattened and elongated, and his jaw widened to accommodate three more rows of teeth and disappeared into his thickening neck. His once cartilaginous (but still human-seeming) nose was now completely flat, bridgeless, and he breathed through two narrowing slits where his nostrils once resided. Small but growing fins tented the fabric of his shirts. Lewis, the man who once gloated about his lack of male pattern baldness, lost every hair on his body in a single week. The gray and white pigmentation of a great white shark emerged, with rapidity, in its place.

Although Wren would never tell him so, Lewis's new eyes disturbed her. Instead of lidded eyes that sank into his face, his evolving, sharkish eyes resembled a black marble resting atop each temple. Without eyelids, he seemed to stare right through her when he slept, like a figure in a painting whose gaze follows you no matter where you orient yourself in the room.

OCTOBER

The administration asked Lewis to resign before the end of the semester "due to a condition which is distracting and distressing for some students." Lewis skimmed the email before going into a four-hour *Our Town* rehearsal and put the bad news aside for a few hours.

When Lewis got home, he exploded.

"It was Colton, the senior who wanted George. Or Kayla, playing Ms. Soames," Lewis vented as a shark tooth fell out of his mouth, pinging on the kitchen floor. "I heard her say she is '*sooooo* tired of playing all the old ladies.' Or, no—"

Lewis paused only to gnaw on a filet of raw salmon, and then he continued ranting with a full mouth:

"No! It's one of the smoking-in-the-parking-lot seniors."

"Lewis, stop," Wren intercepted. "We have no idea who it was. For all we know, the complaint came from a parent, school board member, or another teacher."

"Well, that makes it *even worse*," replied Lewis, punctuating his frustration by slapping the filet on the kitchen table. "I could sue for discrimination! *Woodard* versus *Dallas ISD*!"

After Lewis settled into his reading chair, his rage subsided, Wren cleaned up the day's debris. She emptied the dustpan into the trash beneath the kitchen sink and paused to examine the fallen tooth as a neutral object. (Lately, Lewis lost teeth like she lost hair in the shower.) The tooth was an inch across and serrated like a steak knife. She ran her thumb over the ridges and realized if she pressed down any harder, the tooth would draw blood.

Then Wren's breath got stuck in her upper chest. She slunk beneath the counter and pressed her back against a cabinet with an instinct to disappear, make herself small. Suddenly, Wren was sixteen again, hiding in her bedroom closet. The clod of her mother's footsteps; the soft edges of hanging clothes; the swish of her mother's flesh against the outside wall; then pounding, scratching, pushing on the door.

She heard a scream but did not realize it was her own.

"Wren?" Lewis called out as he hobbled to the kitchen, forgetting his cane. "Are you okay?"

Lewis knelt by her side. This was not the first time something like this had happened.

He put his hand on her back. "It's just me. It's just me, Lewis. It's all safe here."

As deeper breaths entered her body, she began to shake and emit tears of relief and release, tears belonging to a younger version of herself. Lewis peeled her off the floor. Her ribs felt like the hard keys of a xylophone. How had she become so thin without him noticing? He needed to remind her to take care of herself, too.

Then Lewis noticed the blood dripping from her clenched fist.

Lewis opened her palm, peeled the tooth from Wren's tense hand, and helped her to a seat at the kitchen table. The smell of blood stirred him inwardly. Wren was drained and silent, except to insist she did not want to go to the emergency room for stitches.

As Wren slept next to him, exhausted, Lewis remained wide awake. He blamed himself for tonight. Worst of all, at the sight of her blood, Lewis had felt hungry.

That night, Lewis acknowledged the growing, impulsive part of himself he could not trust or control. Its presence made him shudder.

As the lingering summer heat eased into comfortable fall days, Lewis's legs began their dramatic transformation. The skin between his inner thighs conjoined, and then the gathering cascaded toward his ankles and feet. He was confined to a wheelchair. To mask his despair about his legs being stuck together, Lewis joked that he was in his merman phase.

But when his leg bones began to agglutinate, starting with his femurs, the joke stopped being funny. His bones were constantly fracturing. Daily living, for Lewis, became an extended groan. And often a shout.

Of all the physical changes in the last seven months, agglutination was by far the most agonizing. Once his femurs, fibulas, tibias, and metatarsals combined, they would begin to articulate in the new formation, a ladder of bones, his shark vertebral column and heterocercal tail.

While his body rearranged itself, Lewis could do nothing but helplessly bear witness to the process. He grieved the end of his bipedal existence and became frustrated when the discomfort distracted him from his projects.

All the hours he spent theorizing about *magic* seemed so naive now. The main ingredient in transformation was not magic. It was pain.

On the second Wednesday in October, Lewis visited a new building in the medical complex, OCEAN 4. Lewis had skipped OCEAN 2–3, which made him feel like time had been stolen from him. There were no more buildings after OCEAN 4.

With this progression, he traded the psychiatrist, neurologist, and rheumatologist for a palliative care nurse who specialized in the final stages of human-animal mutations. Nurse Tammy, with the spiky, frosted-tipped hair of a nineties boy-band member, spoke to Wren as pain seized Lewis in frequent intervals.

"I'll fill a prescription for a week's worth of oxycodone, and he can take it as needed."

"Does he need to take it with food?" asked Wren, who was typing notes with her laptop.

"*If Lewis is conscious, he needs to be eating,*" Nurse Tammy pressed. "I know it's a challenge to keep up with the feeding schedule, but at this stage, it is critically important for both of your well-being and safety."

A spear of pain struck Lewis where his knees would be. Lewis rocked, and his eyes rolled back in his head.

"You should pick up the prescription before you go home today. And please do not hesitate to call if you need anything. This stage can be unpredictable, and it is my job to make sure Lewis develops as much as he can with as little pain as possible until he's strong enough, as a great white, to live in the ocean."

"Do you think Nurse Tammy showed her hairdresser a picture of Nick Carter or Justin Timberlake?" Lewis asked, perking up on the way home.

Then they both busted out laughing, the kind of whole-body laughter with its own lifespan, laughter guffawing at itself, laughter that made one involuntarily cry, laughter that took one's breath away. Wren pulled over at a car dealership until she was gathered enough to drive.

The rest of the way home, Lewis was lucid and talkative. Wren seized this moment to summarize the appointment.

"Nurse Tammy said you might not recognize me. Soon you might not know who I am."

"Didn't the neurologist say there's a chance that recognition would not be affected?" Lewis asked, recalling something said months ago.

"I think we should prepare." She implied *for the worst*.

"If I forget who you are, maybe you can just remind me."

"And how would I remind you?"

"Maybe just tell me your name,
and ask me to repeat it back.
Once I hear myself say it,
I'm sure I will remember."

"*My name is Wren. Will you say my name?*
Like that?"

"Exactly. Like that."

An incessant desire for fish became louder than all the things Lewis treasured: the heartbeat of language, the idea of living in a tree, the universal within the poetic, and his soft way of loving her.

Without near-constant feeding, Lewis became one with an irascible, symphonic rage.

And this was the best of it.

Wren and Lewis turned off their porch lights on Halloween. They did not need any more frightening things.

The last few weeks had been so difficult, with Lewis coiled on the bathroom floor, screaming, gasping, and moaning as his bone structure reached completion.

Wren was watching a true-crime documentary when Lewis wheeled into the living room, up without Wren's help for the first time in days. She turned off the TV.

"Are you feeling better? Are you hungry?"

Lewis ignored her question. "I had two epiphanies."

"Yeah?"

"In a hundred years, we'll all be dead."

"This is true."

"And you know in eighth-grade science class, when they teach you that matter is not created or destroyed? Only rearranged? Well, personally . . ." Lewis paused. (Was *personally* still a word he could use? Was he still a person?)

"What?" asked Wren.

"Maybe we need to know these things young, because maybe *we're* the matter being rearranged. Maybe it's *us*."

"You and me?"

"I hope."

A BRIEF NOTE ABOUT THE POWER OF FOOD

Consider this image a glimpse of what's to come:

Lewis ate with his whole body, gnashing at raw tuna, salmon, swordfish, and tilapia. He chewed and slurped while his upper body undulated over the kitchen table. Wren soon gave up on plates and served him on baking sheets. Then Wren relinquished baking sheets and served him on the bare table. Finally, she fed him on the floor, which was most comfortable for Lewis, given the fact of his fast-diminishing arms, and for Wren, it was easiest to clean.

She stayed with him all day and night, tending to his feedings. She slept in twenty-minute intervals. Each morning, she went to the grocery store.

SCENE: The Fish Counter

WREN: I'll have everything on the right. Please.

FISH COUNTER GUY: The entire case?

WREN: Yes, please.

FISH COUNTER GUY: You opening a restaurant, ma'am?

WREN: My husband is on a strict diet.

FISH COUNTER GUY: Is your husband a blue whale?

WREN: Just wrap it all up. Please.

FISH COUNTER GUY: Yes, ma'am.

NOVEMBER

Wren and Lewis attended the final performance of *Our Town*, a Sunday matinee.

During the play, Lewis couldn't just be an audience member. He wanted to direct. So he took labored notes in the dark with his good hand, flipping pages in his reporter's notebook. Wren did not stop him, even after a woman whipped her head back, twice, to demonstrate her irritation.

Just as the actress playing Rebecca said her line about the moon exploding, the woman turned around a third time, craning her head and body over the seat.

"*STOP*," she mouthed.

A disco ball lowered from the proscenium arch to represent the moon, and mirrored light twinkled upon the first few rows.

It was then that the woman saw Lewis's angular gray-and-white face, lidless blue-black eyes, and razor-sharp teeth. Horrified, she grabbed her purse and moved briskly to the exit.

"Pearl clutcher," Lewis muttered under his breath.

A few parents and teachers said hello at intermission, but most kept their distance, pretending they did not see him. Then the replacement theater teacher came out from backstage to introduce himself.

During his interview, the would-be replacement, Pierce Anthony, had mentioned how he loved prestigious television dramas, and because of this, he felt equipped to direct a high school play. The interview panel, the principal, the guidance counselor, and the varsity baseball coach who moonlighted as the American history teacher, hired Pierce for enthusiasm rather than experience.

"Pierce Anthony," he said, extending his hand to shake before realizing Lewis's right hand was a pectoral fin with a few errant, dangling fingers. Pierce debated reaching for Lewis's left hand, which, aside from the discoloration, seemed human enough to shake. Lewis held his stare and let Pierce stew in awkwardness as he retracted his hand.

"I have to say, you did great work with the students. Great group," Pierced attempted.

"I know," Lewis replied, returning to his notes and ending the conversation.

"Are you hungry? I have shrimp in the ice chest in the backseat," Wren asked on the way home from the play.

"No."

"Thirsty?"

"No."

"How is the pain?"

"Fine."

. . .

"Well, what did you think of the play?"

"It was an atrocity."

"I thought it was lovely. It had moments."

"Please don't say that."

"I'm sorry."

"Do you honestly think my entire teaching career was for nothing?"

"That's not what I meant, Lewis."

"That's what you seem to be implying."

"I know you would have done better. I'm just saying it wasn't all bad."

"The replacement destroyed the play."

"Well, the young man who played George wept after Emily died. I thought he was impressive."

"It was forced. I would have directed him otherwise."

That night, Lewis parked his wheelchair at the kitchen table and painstakingly typed a written invective to Pierce, whom he now exclusively referred to as The Ignoramus.

Dear Mr. Anthony,

 Wilder writes: "an empty stage in half-light" and "No Curtain. No scenery." Given this, why did you add props? And a set?

 Why were some actors reading from scripts during the performance? The only worse offense would be directing the entire cast to parade across the stage yelling MACBETH *at the top of their lungs. The actors should have been off-book no later than the beginning of the fourth week of rehearsal. You must really push them. Everyone can memorize. Don't take their excuses.*

 Which brings me to my third point. Why did the cast change completely in the third act? High school theater does not thrive on a charity model. A good director treats the cast members as equals while knowing every actor is not.

 Charity casting has major consequences. For example: a false sense of talent and possibility. And thus the willful desire to move to New York, the cruel machine of luck and nepotism.

 Please understand the gravity of your choices.

 In summation: You, sir, are beyond idiocy. You are an ignoramus.

Sincerely,

Lewis Woodard

"Hey, Wren! Come here. I need you to read this!"

After she read Lewis's email to The Ignoramus, she looked up, tired.

"What do you think?" he asked.

"It's a bit mean."

"Good."

"If you are going to ask me if I think you should send this, my answer is I think you should sleep on it."

"I was going to ask you if I left anything out."

Wren shook her head.

And with his good left hand, Lewis hit *send*.

SCENE: Bathtub Conversation

Lewis sits in a wheelchair outside the bathroom while Wren pours a bag of salt into the bathwater. She moves his nightstand next to the bathtub. Wren helps Lewis into the tub. A bit of water overflows. Last, she positions his head on an inflatable pool toy serving as a pillow.

WREN: Would you like your book?

LEWIS: No, thank you.

WREN: But you always read before bed.

LEWIS: I don't feel like reading.

WREN: Are you sure?

LEWIS: Yes.

WREN: If you're not comfortable, one of those airplane pillows might work better.

LEWIS: I'm *fine*, Wren.

WREN: Why are you yelling at me?

LEWIS: I'm not yelling.

WREN: It feels like yelling.

LEWIS: Maybe if you weren't hovering over me all the time, it wouldn't be so loud.

WREN: What has happened to you?

LEWIS: I think we both know what "happened" to me.

. . .

WREN: Do you care if I watch *Game of Thrones* without you this time?

LEWIS: You can do whatever you like.

Lewis wished he were writing rather than sitting alone in the bathtub. He still felt a story trapped inside him. He told Wren he'd stopped writing due to his diminishing motor skills. He did not tell her that he also couldn't get past the shapes of the letters to remember what he wanted to communicate with them.

For example, *A* went up steeply, peaked at the top, and tumbled dramatically downward. *O* was the most consistent, unstoppable, and tireless of all the letters, yet not as balanced as his sister *Q*. *I* and *J* belonged together as either siblings or longtime lovers. While *J* teetered on a rocking chair–like foundation, enjoying the playful quality of being chronically imbalanced, sturdy *I* took up as little space as possible. Lewis had a new understanding for what it meant to be lost in a story.

As Lewis became disenfranchised from the only symbols he had to describe reality, he felt similarly unreal to himself.

His friends stopped texting and calling. His own mother couldn't look at him without crying. His father stood six feet away even though Lewis's condition was not contagious. Wren was the only person left who still approached Lewis as he once was. Did she not see how the man she married was already irretrievable despite himself? Lewis hoped she wouldn't be the last to know.

SCENE: Bathtub Conversation, Part II

Wren taps lightly on the bathroom door.

LEWIS: Come in.

Wren enters.

LEWIS: How was *Game of Thrones*?

WREN: Somebody died.

LEWIS: Don't tell me who.

WREN: I won't.

. . .

LEWIS: Could we cuddle?

WREN: In the bathtub?

LEWIS: Sure.

Wren undresses and steps into the tub. To Lewis, she seems new again, like Salad Girl, their first meeting at the café.

WREN: What are you smiling about?

LEWIS: You.

Wren puts her head on his chest and wraps her arms around his shoulders. She traces his dorsal fin with her fingertips.

WREN: Does it hurt?

LEWIS: Not much. Just a little tender.

. . .

WREN: What do you think about us having a baby?

LEWIS: Really? Now? Are you serious?

Wren shakes her head.

WREN: I just wanted to know what it felt like to ask the question.

LEWIS: I'm sorry.

WREN: I should go to bed.

LEWIS: Stay, just another minute.

Wren paid their neighbor's nephews thirty dollars to set up an above-ground pool while Lewis's dad took him to see Nurse Tammy, and afterward, Wren dumped six bags of rock salt into the pool as the garden hose filled it very slowly.

"What do you think? It's saltwater," she said when Lewis got home.

"This was unnecessary. But thank you."

"Try it out."

Lewis hoisted himself onto the ladder with his remaining hand and forearm and swung his tail back and forth until he had enough momentum to fling himself into the water.

"How does it feel?" she asked.

"Very nice," Lewis replied.

"Are you humoring me?"

"No. This is really wonderful. Thank you."

Truly: It was the most comfortable he'd been in months. Lewis floated in the pool all afternoon as the water continued to rise.

Meanwhile, he discovered that his vision, while deteriorating in the open air, was perfectly clear underwater. His fins were useless in his life above the water, but in the pool, they worked like rudders. Gills cut his chest laterally, shuttering open and closed as he took big satisfying breaths.

When the pool was full to the brim many hours later, Lewis swam around and around and around and around, as he did with his friends when he was boy, creating a cyclone with his own unleashed energy.

When Wren came out to bring him in for the evening, Lewis said he wanted to spend the night in the pool.

"Are you sure? You don't want to sleep in the bathtub?"

"This is good. I'll throw a pebble at the bedroom window if I want to come in," Lewis joked, but Wren did not laugh.

Wren put his wheelchair next to the pool and a stack of towels and three salmon fillets on the platform at the top of the ladder—*for later if you feel hungry*.

That night, Lewis rested very well.

Wren did not sleep at all.

When the Tiny Pregnant Woman went on bed rest, she texted Wren that they would no longer be able to swim together. Then, in her dry, declarative way, she invited Wren to visit her twice a week at home.

The Tiny Pregnant Woman resided in a stark three-thousand-square-foot penthouse in Preston Hollow, coincidentally, the same building as Wren's boss, Jonathan, who hosted an annual holiday dinner party for the team at his condo on the third floor.

Wren rang the bell in the familiar dim hallway, and the Tiny Pregnant Woman opened the heavy front door, wearing a floor-length linen robe. Her belly was not soft and globular. Instead, it was pointed like the tied end of a balloon.

"Hello," the Tiny Pregnant Woman said, expressionless. "Thank you for coming. I missed you."

"Oh, you're welcome," Wren replied, surprised by the Tiny Pregnant Woman's vulnerable admission. "I've missed you, too."

"That's nice," the Tiny Pregnant Woman replied, once again withdrawing.

The foyer opened into a gallery-like living room with floor-to-ceiling windows on one wall and a contemporary triptych on the other. The minimal furniture with right angles, stone surfaces, and uniformly low profiles seemed designed for the space rather than the people who lived in it. Also, the marble floors, white walls, and view of the sky made Wren feel like she was inside a cloud.

"Would you like anything to drink?" the Tiny Pregnant Woman asked as they passed a stainless-steel refrigerator built into the wall near a bench with elaborate geometric carvings.

"No, thank you."

As Wren followed the Tiny Pregnant Woman down a spacious hallway lit from above with skylights, what interested Wren more than the unique architecture and furnishings was the Tiny Pregnant Woman's surprising proclivity for literary whimsy. The complete works of Charles Dickens with rainbow spines lined the mantel in the study. Jane Austen quotes were printed on the bathroom wallpaper. A *James and the Giant Peach* movie poster hung in the screening room. When they passed a Wonderland-themed nursery, the Tiny Pregnant Woman abruptly shut off the lights and closed the door.

"The housekeeper never turns off the lights," the Tiny Pregnant Woman said, walking faster and looking straight ahead so Wren could not see her flushed face.

Wren sat in a bright yellow ball chair from the 1970s in a far corner of the bedroom, the only seating other than the Tiny Pregnant Woman's bed, a thin mattress atop a bamboo platform rising just a few inches off the floor. The Tiny Pregnant Woman groaned as she lowered herself with a deep squat. Then she explained her situation, referring to herself in third person as *the mother:*

"The mother can only have juice, seeds, and poultry," the Tiny Pregnant Woman said as she poured herself a glass of cranberry juice from a carafe sitting on a Z-shaped nightstand.

"A decreased appetite indicates the falcon twins, the eyases, are strong enough to claw, peck, and scratch themselves out of the mother's womb. The eyases will emulate the hatching process by incorrectly assuming the mother's body is an eggshell, creating an orifice to exit anywhere they see fit.

"For this reason, bird pregnancies are often fatal to the mother, and the mother should not deny this possibility. She should plan for two outcomes: death and living in an impaired body.

"If the birds mangle my spinal cord, I've told my husband to pull the plug," the Tiny Pregnant Woman concluded, jarringly reverting to the first person in such a confident cadence that Wren thought the Tiny Pregnant Woman had rehearsed the sentence. "Anyway, how is Lewis?"

Wren tried to match her confidence. "We moved him to a pool in the backyard. He's breathing much better now."

"That's nice."

"Yes, and I've been waiting to tell you: I'm working out a plan. A plan to be with him. I haven't told anyone yet."

Then Wren explained her idea with an optimism that annoyed the Tiny Pregnant Woman, who missed her fellow melancholy friend. Besides, she thought Wren's idea was desperate and poorly planned.

"Birds fly. Fish swim. You need to give Lewis the freedom to occupy the right domain. The same goes for you."

"You don't know my husband."

"You don't know how the world works."

The Tiny Pregnant Woman's marriage had a culture of sacrifice rather than compromise. For this reason, she was jealous of Lewis, even though she had never met him, because he had a partner like Wren.

"You should go. I need to rest. Let yourself out. The door will lock behind you," the Tiny Pregnant Woman concluded flatly.

With no large fanfare, this interaction concluded Wren and the Tiny Pregnant Woman's unusual friendship.

They each served a purpose in the other's life, and separately, each had enough to grieve without grieving each other as well. The Tiny Pregnant Woman had already surrendered to a fatalistic future, but Wren still had hope.

As the gate of the Tiny Pregnant Woman's building released Wren into a crisp autumn afternoon, she marveled at her new, uncharacteristic optimism. When did she become such a dreamer? And how? Well, deep down, she knew.

Lewis was a magician, performing trick after marvelous trick, misdirecting her attention with jokes, stories, and games. As Wren fell for the distractions, Lewis tattooed her with beautiful poetry in a place she would never see but somehow read every second.

After Wren parked in the driveway of the home they'd chosen for its balance of style and functionality, a rumble in her gut ricocheted through her chest and threatened to blast open her controlled exterior. Wren noted the time on the dash and decided to let herself cry but only for three minutes. After checking to make sure a neighbor wasn't watching, Wren lowered her forehead to the steering wheel, wrapped her arms tightly around her torso, and wept.

After what happens next, most would say Lewis took a turn. Maybe not yet for the worst, because definitions of right and wrong, good and bad, light and dark become more nebulous and subjective in uncommon circumstances. Meanwhile, winter revealed itself in small, biting glimpses.

After sighting Lewis at the final performance of *Our Town,* a few of his former colleagues wanted to organize a commemorative celebration while there was still time. The secretaries in the principal's office, typically tasked with planning retirement parties as well as the annual Secret Santa game, decided *Send-off* was the least egregious option for the invitation's subject line. (*Going Away* and *We'll Miss You* did not sit well with the principal, because they "alluded too much to the tragic situation.")

On the day of the party, Lewis struggled to put on a shirt with his remaining, yet diminished, arm. He looked less like an unwell man and more like a malnourished great white shark—small and gaunt at just over five feet tall with a bony vertebral column.

Wren watched as Lewis fumbled with the tiny buttons.

"Do you need help?" she asked, knowing what his answer would be.

First silence, as Lewis uncharacteristically considered accepting Wren's help. Then a swift horizontal headshake, *no*.

There were too many people and chairs for the size of the room, and Lewis's wheelchair fit only next to the doorway. As a result, anyone entering the lounge hit Lewis's back wheels with the door, and anyone leaving felt obliged to divulge to him why.

The red, yellow, and blue decor in the teachers' lounge, reminiscent of a child's birthday party, contradicted the gathering's anxious, somber mood. People spoke in soft voices and approached Lewis armed with rehearsed statements of gratitude and platitudes laced with Christian undertones. They did not let their eyes explore what they really wanted to see: Lewis's grotesque form.

They had all heard of cases like this, but seeing a Carcharodon carcharias mutation in real life was as uncommon as encountering a movie star in a rural town or a rare fossil in one's own backyard. It was unfortunate, they murmured, that such a delightful soul would endure this much darkness; that such a creative, visionary person would be left with nothing and no one in the end.

Beyond pity, grief, and secret fascination, almost everyone at the party discovered the same private truth: Lewis and Wren's situation made them feel better about themselves. Afterward, as those in attendance sifted through their own junk drawer of troubles, they would thank the tilted universe it wasn't their change to bear; their blood and bones ripping away from humanity's known, narrow lane; their life and family broken and rearranged.

The most senior secretary busied herself by cutting the supermarket sheet cake into a grid, putting each small square on a bright yellow dessert plate. But no one was interested in eating cake, and the plates crowded the table, untouched.

Noticing the secretary's distress at the fact that no one was eating any cake, the geometry teacher began handing out plates, forks, and napkins, saving Lewis the piece with theater masks piped in black and red buttercream. Lewis took a bite for show, gagged, and spit up on the floor. (People

136

food did not sit well with him anymore.) Wren knelt to clean it up while everyone tried to ignore the string of saliva spooling from Lewis's mouth and onto the back of Wren's blouse.

Through all of this, Pierce Anthony's was the loudest voice in the room.

Lewis is right, Wren thought. *He really is The Ignoramus.*

Wren saw Lewis's relaxed expression contort to revulsion when The Ignoramus began a proud retelling of his recent directorial debut.

The party would not end well.

SCENE: Lewis's Final Lecture, "Artistic Integrity in the Dallas Independent School District"

LEWIS: Did you receive my email?

THE IGNORAMUS: I did. I'm sorry you did not like the play. It was my first time directing. I suppose I'm learning, too.

The lights dim to give the illusion of the walls growing tighter on Lewis and The Ignoramus. The room grows quiet. Wren steps forward and tries to stop Lewis by squeezing his shoulder. But Lewis jerks away and almost tips over in his wheelchair.

LEWIS: I expect an apology.

THE IGNORAMUS: With all due respect, sir. I didn't do anything to you.

Lewis slaps The Ignoramus in the face with his tail. The Ignoramus's jaw dislocates and dangles as blood waterfalls over his lower lip. Lewis smacks The Ignoramus again, this time slicing the back of his neck. The Ignoramus drops to his knees as blood capes his back and shoulders. The assistant principal, a portly man who never moved so quickly in all his life, tries to pull Lewis away. Then Lewis tail-slaps the assistant principal, too, and he falls into a huddle of teachers who fall like dominoes. Someone screams, "Call 911!" Blackout.

Lewis observed his actions as if he were watching a movie. He hovered above himself, personally detached yet rapt in the plot. The being before him was not the person he knew himself to be, and at the same time, he understood his new self completely. These movements came from a natural place of yearning, like that for sex, food, sleep, or warmth. It was both excruciating and exhilarating to have so little control.

Wren's voice brought him back.

"Lewis, please. Please, Lewis. Stop, Lewis, please."

Lewis's consciousness snapped back into his body, and he saw the blood, the paramedics, the police, and most alarmingly, Wren. She wore the fragmented expression of a child lost in a surging crowd.

Then he left his body, again taking a spectator's view. For the first time in his life, Lewis was not the main character, reality's most reliable witness. This was Wren's story, and he saw everything through her eyes.

He saw Wren's horror as he threatened the colleagues he once made laugh in staff meetings. He watched her watch him writhe on the floor as three burly policemen tried to pin him down, smearing blood—some of The Ignoramus's but mostly his own—all over the tile. He watched her watch him receive tranquilizer injections until he could no longer claw, bite, slap, or scream. At last, he witnessed Wren, his assiduous, loving partner, see him not for what he was but for what he had become.

Lewis's nightmares were now in full bloom.

His wife loved him, but she was also terrified of him.

And then everything went dark.

Lewis was unconscious when they got home, but when he awoke, he began slamming himself into the refrigerator and kitchen table, tearing cabinets from their hinges, and throwing knives into the wall like darts.

Wren locked herself in the bedroom. Outside the door, it sounded like an ongoing collision.

The literature with recommendations for caregivers said to remain calm and seek shelter: *A mutating person is not in control of their actions, just as someone having a seizure is often unable to communicate that they are having one.* The literature did not tell her what to think about or how to feel.

Wren sat on the floor at the foot of their bed, put her head between her knees, closed her eyes, and sifted through extinct versions of herself: the girl riding the mechanical pony outside the grocery store, the movement knotting her hair into rat's nests that would be tugged out later with a strong comb; the teenager studying hard, not primarily for the acquisition of knowledge but for the opportunity to convince a better place she belonged; the young woman who tripped into a love she was not ready for and became convinced it was strangling her; the woman who wanted to build a life with a man who pulled her into his warm current and vowed never to let go, a man who taught her how to notice beauty and convinced her she was worthy of it, too.

The thought that she needed to call Nurse Tammy interrupted the memory stream, but Wren's phone was in her purse, which was hanging by the front door. She'd have to pass by the kitchen and her carnivorous husband to retrieve it.

A metal crash. Wren felt the house rattle. Lewis screamed. What could she do for him that would not endanger and possibly hurt herself in the process?

Only heaven can help him, said a mysterious voice in her head. It couldn't be her own. Wren did not believe in God, much less heaven. The next possibility was that she might be remembering her mother. Angela believed in a plethora of invisible things, just like Lewis. Wren missed her mother most at times like these, when she felt powerless and had no idea what to do. She looked at her hands as if an answer were written upon them.

Then Wren had an epiphany, an insight, a gift that would carry her through yet another difficult day.

The surface of love was a feeling, but beyond this thin layer, there was a fathomless, winding maze of caverns offering many places to see and explore. Wren used to think romantic passion only grew more intense in the depths. But this belief was naive and impractical, a by-product of a certainty-obsessed culture that equates love with longing and views ambivalence as a fatal flaw.

Wren saw now how passion was delicate and temporary, a visitor, a feeling that would come and go. Feelings fled under pressure; feelings did not light the darkness. What remained strong in the deep, the hard times, was love as an effort, a doing, a conscious act of will. Soulmates, like her and Lewis, were not theoretical and found. They were tangible, built.

When it was quiet outside the bedroom door, Wren stepped into the kitchen to survey the damage, which was worse than she expected.

Lewis had managed to tear off the refrigerator handle and throw it through the window above the kitchen sink. A variety of punctures in the wall exposed drywall and insulation. A fist-sized dent on the dishwasher door. A splintered dining room chair in the kitchen sink. Shattered glass: plates, mugs, spice jars, condiments. The light fixture above the dining room table, dangling in shards. His wheelchair, shunned in the hallway, banged up but still usable. Lewis himself, draped across the table, unconscious with his now customary open-eyed look. A sleeping Venus.

In the wake of this chaos, Wren had another flashback, one she had not entered in years. She was twenty-two, visiting her mother at the facility. The only recognizable part of her mother's demeanor was the way she turned her head to notice Wren when she entered. In those moments, Wren always imagined her mother was smiling at her, wanting to say, *How wonderful of you to stop by.*

*   *   *

After Lewis was comfortable in the pool, too exhausted and stunned to be apologetic, Wren called Nurse Tammy.

"It's time to let him go," Nurse Tammy said after Wren recounted the going-away party and Lewis's episode.

"But he's never been violent before, never in his life," Wren implored, momentarily forgetting the day they both got banned from the zoo.

"I'm very sorry, but I am required to report this incident. You must release him in a habitable environment within three weeks or the government will do it for you."

"I'll do it," Wren heard herself say. "As soon as possible."

The next morning, the principal called to express his concern and share that Pierce's injuries required stitches but were, in the long term, not serious.

"After everything," the principal added, "Pierce said he doesn't want to press charges. Remarkable young man. He said he feels so terribly for you."

"Thank you," Wren said with a growing pit in her stomach. "Tell him thank you."

Wren, age twenty

After days of driving from New England to California, the destination was anticlimactic. Wren had thought California would be all blue skies and warm sepia sunshine, but on that day, it was just as gray as the Northeast. It was too cold to swim, so Rachel and Wren dipped their toes in the water and ran up the beach when the tides came up past their ankles. Then they looked at the tide pool creatures and strolled a couple miles along the ridge above the beach.

"Are we okay?" Rachel asked when they stopped to sit on a bench at a scenic overlook.

The scent of marijuana wafted in their direction, its source unknown. Wren drew a circle in the dirt with her sneaker.

"Yes. Of course," Wren answered automatically.

"You've been somewhere else for a few days."

"I'm here."

"Mentally?"

Wren concentrated on her circle, making the trench deeper and deeper.

"I'm right here. And I'm not going anywhere," she said, feeling less sure of the statement after she said it.

In preparation for their encroaching departure and Lewis's release, Wren ventured to a lakeside beach in pouring rain. She hauled the gear, including an oxygen tank she'd just filled at the dive shop, to the freestanding concrete bathroom.

Wren struggled to get into the wetsuit. She googled instructions for putting on the rest.

Everything Wren wore was a combination of heavy, cumbersome, or tight. The tank alone felt like a whole other person on her back. Wearing the flippers, Wren took knee-high steps to the end of the pier before she realized scooting forward without picking up her feet was much easier.

On Wren's first attempt, her mask filled with water.

On her second, she descended too quickly and felt a sharp pain in her right ear.

On her third, Wren dropped smoothly into the dark lake without a glitch. The ease felt accidental, especially because lately, much simpler things seemed to be extraordinarily hard. For the first time in months, she was weightless.

As Wren stood on the murky lake bottom, she realized the mask was pointless. The world was mud. Then the roiling thoughts: *What if, what if, what if, what if?*

What if it was Wren who left the known world first? What if that was the surprise, the plot twist? If her equipment malfunctioned, would she asphyxiate and lose consciousness? What if she passed into the next plane right then and there, in the lake? What if the solution to life, which seemed so often like an ongoing series of hardships, was to abandon it?

The local police would find Wren's abandoned car, and then rescue divers, her body. Lewis would have to identify her, but maybe that would be the exact moment he stopped remembering. He'd tell the police officer through rows of pointed, sharp teeth: *I've never seen that face in my life.*

A week before Thanksgiving, Lewis said goodbye to his family in the back-yard of his boyhood home. He wanted to see the live oaks one more time. Afterward, Greg checked the tire pressure on the car, and Annie packed a cooler full of tuna for Lewis, fruit for Wren, and two batches of brownies she'd baked at three o'clock in the morning because she couldn't sleep or stop crying. The past two weeks, Lewis was the only one of them who had been hungry.

"Are you sure you don't want your father and me to come?" Annie asked as tears made tracks in yesterday's makeup.

"We should be all right," Wren answered for both of them.

Lewis's breathing was shallow and raspy, and it hurt to speak, but he wished he'd planned a few words to say, a speech of hope and gratitude. At the end, he would recite one of his favorite Eugene O'Neill lines: *It was a great mistake, my being born a man, I would have been much more successful as a seagull or a fish.*

Instead, he was dizzy, losing his sense of place. Light. Heat. Concrete. Grass. Car. House. Sky. Who were these sad people staring at him, asking him questions using words he did not understand? He looked to Wren to remember. He always remembered Wren.

Traveling through Texas and New Mexico, Lewis was quiet, except for his squeezed inhalations and rattled exhales. Wren had removed two rows of seats and stretched a tarp across the back to keep Lewis from getting stuck, essentially Velcroed, to the SUV's polyester lining.

Meanwhile, Wren rehearsed the plan in her head. It would all be revealed to Lewis soon. She told herself everything would work out. It had to. Doubt had no place here, not now.

"Where are we?" croaked Lewis as the vehicle came to a stop after an eleven-hour driving day.

"A Best Western in Albuquerque. Home for the night." Wren turned around and saw canned tuna smeared all over Lewis, the tarp, and even, somehow, the lower part of the windows. Lewis hadn't eaten any of his dinner.

"What time is it?" Lewis asked. The digital clock on the dashboard was a blur of dark fractals.

"Just after midnight. Do you want to stay in the backseat tonight? Or in the hotel room?"

Wren left Lewis in the shower with the cold water running, wiped down the back of the SUV, and refilled the ice chests from the hotel's ice machine. She noticed her stomach growling for the first time in days and remembered Annie's brownies. She made a final trip to the car, ignoring the front-desk person looking upon her with both curiosity and sympathy.

Back in the room, Wren took three bites, crawled under the comforter, and collapsed, surrendering, at last, to slumber.

Wren stalled by spreading the trip across as many days as possible. Lewis knew this with complete certainty after they spent a full day at the Grand Canyon, Wren pushing his chair on accessible nature paths while people gawked at them.

O n the fifth day of the journey, Lewis began to hallucinate.

iPhone-sized insects with long black antennae and macabre red eyes populated the ceiling of the car, whispering to one another in their own guttural language. When the vehicle shifted, Lewis slid across the tarp and pressed against the side of the vehicle. Then the insects would scamper down to bite him on his fins as a punishment for invading their territory.

"Hey! Argh!" Lewis shouted. "GET OFF ME!"

"What's going on?" Wren said. "Are you getting too warm? Are you hungry?"

But Lewis did not respond. He was already unreachable, lost in another hallucination.

On the sixth and final day of the journey, Lewis had four visions. In each vision, he could walk around and experience reality as he once had, standing tall at five feet eleven inches with four limbs and a set of easy-breathing human lungs.

The first vision was a memory. Ambushed by infatuation, Lewis told his parents during a Sunday dinner how he had just met the woman he wanted to marry. His mother almost dropped her fork.

"How long have you been seeing her?" asked Greg.

"Seventeen days."

"What is her name?" asked Annie.

"Wren."

"Wren?" his mother repeated.

"Wren, like the bird," Lewis replied.

Then his parents said her name together as if to feel a fraction of their son's new love move through them. *Wren.*

The second vision was a revised recollection of the strawberry moon night, his masterpiece memory enlivened. This version of the memory contained no illness, no impending dissolution of his humanity, no chasm splintering him from his wife, his life at an unstoppable rate—just another repeatable beautiful night.

The third vision involved the closing night of *Our Town*. This production of the play was flawless, Lewis's precise directorial vision.

In the final scene of the play, when the ghost of Emily Gibbs visits her twelfth birthday, the theater hums with presence as everyone in the audience and cast alike remembers that joy and grief are human birthrights, but mostly, being alive is everything in between.

After the Stage Manager leads Emily Gibbs back to the cemetery, he looks directly into the audience at Lewis. The play is not over yet.

SCENE: Lewis's Fourth Vision

Lewis rises from his seat, and as he does, the high school auditorium trans-forms into the Broadhurst Theatre, where Lewis saw his first Broadway play, The Tempest, *at age fourteen. The actor playing the Stage Manager on the previous page is no longer a teenager but, rather, Sir Patrick Stewart.*

PATRICK STEWART: The stage is all yours.

LEWIS: Sir Patrick Stewart? Are you talking to me?

PATRICK STEWART: Who else would it be?

Lewis makes his way through the audience, down the aisle of the Broad-hurst, and up the stairs to the stage.

PATRICK STEWART: We have been waiting for you, Lewis Woodard.

Patrick Stewart exits stage left, and Lewis finds his light downstage center. He looks down, focusing his energy like he used to do before an audition monologue. But this is no audition. When Lewis looks up, the house is packed with everyone he has ever known.

LEWIS: Goodbye to continents and Shakespeare.
    Goodbye to bed and sleeping with both eyes closed.

Goodbye to holding hands and bare feet in soft grass.
Goodbye to the roads, paths, trails, and I-40 West,
which have all carried me
to here and this.
Are we all just actors, performing some unbound art form for God,
the audience of space?
I wish I could have seen then
what I know now.
All along, I had the starring role.

Lewis takes time to really see his body, starting with his hands. He appreciates every joint, bone, and fold of skin. Then he takes three steps backward into the darkness.

LEWIS: Mr. Stewart, I'm ready. Take me to the sea.

For three beats, the audience remains silent, breathing with Lewis, forgetting about time, tomorrow, and trouble. Then they leap to their feet. A standing ovation. Blackout.

When Lewis and Wren arrived at the beach, the same beach she and Rachel had visited on her college trip fifteen years ago, Wren realized she'd planned for everything except how to get Lewis from the car to the ocean. She was momentarily annoyed with herself for not utilizing the practical advantages of choosing a familiar place.

With the trunk open, Wren pulled Lewis toward the back of the vehicle by tugging on the tarp. When Lewis was at the edge, she tried to ease him onto the ground gently, tail first, but he slid out quickly, his head landing on the concrete with a hard thud. Lewis groaned.

"God, Lewis. I'm so sorry."

She began to drag the tarp, with Lewis atop it, across the bike path and down the beach. She stopped just before the shoreline.

"I need something from the car. Wait here," Wren said, panting.

Lewis nodded and watched her sprint, sand flying in her wake. He couldn't go anywhere, anyway.

A few minutes later, Wren stood before him in scuba diving gear. Lewis felt a reflexive surge of delight. Of course: Wren had a plan for everything. And then Lewis's heart began to break.

"I'm coming with you, Lewis.
I'll take care of all the arrangements.
Leave you here for a few days.
Go back to Dallas.
Sell the house.
Buy a boat.
As you know,
I lived on a houseboat until I was ten years old.
It would be like,
like coming home.
We will explore the ocean together,
and build a life we never imagined."

Lewis found himself in an unusual position. He was typically the one with impossible ideas, trying to convince Wren of their feasibility. Now he knew what it felt like to be on the other side. He wanted to argue with her, tell her it might be dangerous for them to be together, that he couldn't count on himself to protect her in the ocean, that he himself might be the danger. At the same time, Lewis felt proud. Wren, his practical, enduring wife, was dreaming.

Together, they forged ahead in the choppy dark water. Lewis darted through the swells while Wren struggled, turning sideways to avoid being knocked off her feet. The ocean's power was far greater than she'd anticipated. In the lake, she was adept but hardly confident. The ocean exposed her inexperience.

Waves rocked her, and she inhaled seawater, coughing. Everything was wrong. She forgot how she was supposed to breathe. Maybe her equipment wasn't working? She lost both flippers and fought to find them in the surf. She would try again after she'd adjusted on the shore. She wouldn't give up easily. It would be fine. It would have to be. This was just the test run. She would tell Lewis she'd anticipated it. Adjustment periods were expected. First-time bumbles were not emblematic of ultimate failure. Plus, there are no oceans near Dallas in which to practice diving properly. Yes, she would get proper training near the boat she had not purchased yet and join him gradually. Lewis would surely understand her dilemma. He was the most understanding person she'd ever met.

Lewis circled back to her.

"Hold on," he said. Wren grabbed his dorsal fin and wrapped her legs around him as if riding a horse.

On shore, she frantically adjusted her equipment. "I lost my flippers. Dammit."

"Hey. Wren." Lewis peered up at her with heavy eyes, his tail in the water and his upper body resting on the angled, wet sand.

"Just give me a second. I'm almost ready," she said.

"Hey, look here, Wren. Let's talk about this."

"*Please*. Give me time."

"Did you do some kind of certification program?" Lewis asked in a flash of human rationality.

"No."

"A class?"

"No!"

"Oh."

"I taught myself."

"Where?"

"Don't worry about it."

"Please stop all this. Just be here with me."

Wren searched Lewis's eyes and spotted a faint glimpse of her husband.

"Oh, Lewis. Your eyes are full of life again."

"You have so much future ahead."

"And I want to spend it with you. This is only the beginning."

"What if this is just the natural order of things? It doesn't mean we don't love each other. Maybe it means we do."

"No. Lewis. Stop. Stop saying those things," Wren pleaded, dropping to her knees, flinging off the oxygen tank, vest, and mask, and latching on to Lewis with both arms just under his pectoral fins to keep him from slipping away.

"Things like this happen to lots of people. Marriages sometimes . . . end. For reasons that have nothing to do with the two people. Sometimes people need different things. You've been a wonderful, *wonderful* wife. My best friend—"

"*No, Lewis.*

I'm going to visit you every day.

And then someday,

when they find a way to reverse your condition

scientifically, medically,

we'll buy some land with wonderful trees and

build treehouses in every one of them.

And we could have a bunch of kids, and

read plays together, as a family,

and on clear nights, we'll look at the stars.

Can you picture it?

And if you decide you don't want kids,

Totally okay, totally fine.

We'll read every book and

watch every show and
sleep in and travel and
make money and art and love
all the time, whenever we want.
Or we could adopt a couple big dogs.
You've always wanted big dogs, right?"

Lewis stared at her blankly as his tail swished in the surf behind him.

"Why aren't you saying anything? Please say something," Wren begged, clutching him harder.

"I'm not the person I used to be. I'm not the man you married."

"What do you mean?"

Lewis wished he could embrace her back, wrap two human arms around her small, shivering frame. He tried to do the best he could with words:

"It's like standing in my childhood bedroom,
looking around at the comic books,
action figures,
and school yearbooks
with signatures from all the girls,
and remembering how that tiny room
used to be my only stake in the world.
I don't know how else to explain it.
There are things I cannot unsee."

Wren felt as if a wet sponge were lodged in her trachea, as if she were breathing underwater. Lewis continued:

"I want you to call my dad if that bathroom faucet starts dripping again.
He helped me fix it in the first place,
but I didn't tell you because
I wanted you to think I was the sort of man who could fix things.
But I'm not that kind of man, and I'm sorry I pretended.
Also, there's a drawer of T-shirts I forgot to donate in the garage.
But it can be nice to have some extra T-shirts
for washing the car."

"You always wash the car," Wren said as she got on her stomach and twined her ankles around his tail, just below his second small dorsal fin, trying to touch as much of him as possible.

"I did. But maybe you'll meet someone . . ."

"No, Lewis. Please—"

"Someone Else who would love to wash it for you."

"Someone Else who would love to wash it for me," Wren echoed as she tried to catch her breath.

"Yes. Someone Else."

"I don't want Someone Else."

"Are you cold?"

"I'm fine."

"It's almost dark now."

"Not quite," Wren said. It seemed the sliver of orange sun over the water was the only entity taking her side. Seawater lapped over their bodies and receded again and again. They were refracted creatures, occupying the vacillating doorway between earthly worlds.

"You've been driving for days. You must be exhausted."

"It was nothing."

"I have to go."

"Lewis, don't you remember our plan?

For when you forget?

My name is Wren. Will you say my name?"

"I have to go."

"Please, Lewis. Just—

say my name."

Lewis thought her name before saying it aloud, realizing for the first time that "Wren, like the bird" was too ordinary a tagline for a person who was so complicated, colorful, surprising, and smart.

"Wren," he said.

"Yes. Again."

"Wren."

"Again."

"Wren."

"Again—

Again—

Again—

Again!

Don't you remember who we are?"

"I haven't forgotten a thing."

As their saltwater tears combined with the sea, Lewis finally understood the log line of their love story: He was an aimless kite in search of a string to ground him to the world, but instead, he'd found Wren, a great, strong wind who supported his exploration of the sky.

"You make everything better than when you found it,
especially me.
Thank you for a wonderful marriage.
I would change nothing, not for anything.
And you deserve much more than the idea of me.
It would stifle your possibility.
When Someone Else comes your way,
you have my blessing, my absolute blessing,
to begin again.
You will be a wonderful mother
and wife.
. . .
You are Wren, the woman of my daydreams.
Wren, the time of my life."

She sat on her knees again, pulling Lewis's head onto her lap while the tide's stronger arm tried to pull him into the ocean. Wren would not let him slip away even as his dermal denticles rubbed her arms raw. Lewis felt the warmth of her thighs beneath his jaw and kissed her knees, wishing there were more he could do, wishing, again, that he could hold her, too.

They continued to sit like this, the chilly Pacific waters caressing legs and tail. (Wren wished they could walk back to the car together, shoulder to shoulder. Afterward, they would eat tacos on a picnic table outside a gas station. Then they would find a beachside motel and leave the window open at night so they could hear the waves while they slept. Maybe they would watch too many episodes of television and make love at two in the morning because they were both awake and why not.) There is never a right time to say goodbye.

Then, for the last time, Lewis lifted his head and kissed her mouth: flower-petal lips to sharp teeth.

"I love you," he said, and mouthed, *Goodbye.*

And in a breath, her arms were empty.

Wren watched him swim into the uncharted blackness with a great new athleticism, rocketing through the surf, suspended like a trapeze artist between air and water.

She remembered what he looked like at home, suffering in a too-small bathtub and, later, an aboveground pool. She'd done her best, and it was not enough.

For hours into the night, Wren stared into the black ocean, waiting for Lewis to come back to her, waiting for him to change his mind. She lost track of time. The stars were insultingly vibrant and still amid such fresh entropy. Overhead, the last quarter-moon gained height, and once again, the heart of Wren's life disassembled.

What do I need? What do I need? What do I need? What do I need? What do I need? Wren asked into the night, just as her mother taught her when she was a small girl.

Finally, an answer appeared:

Everything,
everything,
everything,
everything,
I need everything,
and could it be that everything
is too much for one woman
to seek and grasp, alone?

Wren woke up the next morning, damp and aching. She waited on the beach until midafternoon—squinty eyes on the horizon line like a sailor's wife—still hoping Lewis would change his mind and come back to her.

Around four o'clock in the afternoon, Wren accepted the facts: Lewis had wanted to leave, and he wasn't coming back for her. Once he decided to do something, he did not give up until he had seen it through. Maybe she was the same. Wren abandoned her equipment on the beach and changed into yesterday's clothes in the back of the SUV. It was done.

Wren's twenties

In the weeks after spring break, Rachel opened herself wide, loving in all the ways she could while Wren retreated further and further away from her, ignoring Rachel's calls and messages and being cold and brief when they did happen to interact.

Rachel initiated the breakup, but it was clearly Wren who wanted it.

"You think you are so wise and experienced. You think you know what life is. But you don't," Rachel said through tears outside the sorority house.

In this self-despising moment, Wren reached for Rachel's hands, suddenly not caring if any of her sorority sisters saw her with a woman. But Rachel pulled away.

"Rachel, I'm sorry. I don't know why I can't— You deserve the world and more. You deserve to be happy." The friction in Wren's inward reality confused her. Yes, she was heartbroken, but a significant part of her was also relieved.

"You're missing the point. I *know* I deserve to be happy. I hope you realize that you do, too. Maybe next time Someone comes around, you'll be ready. Maybe next time, you'll understand."

After college, Wren set out to build the opposite life of her childhood. She chose a career in finance because she was good with numbers and wanted to make a lot of money. Numbers provided certainty. Certainty provided control. Control provided protection.

Predictably, she excelled. The pace, pressure, and precision forced Wren to forget everything else in her life. Work was the drug she loved, and she loved nothing else. She racked up promotions and bonuses. She made obscene money and spent very little of it. She slept only when her body would no longer hold her up. By the time she moved to Dallas a few months shy of twenty-four, Wren was making more money in a single year than her mother earned in ten.

But no amount of work or money would numb the shame and regret Wren carried about being largely absent during her mother's final days. Wren did not know then how precious time was or how four words could crush a person, especially if they came from the person they loved most.

In a world without her mother, Wren found herself imprisoned in a flulike loneliness. Work was no longer enough to sustain her. She needed people. Wren thought often of Rachel's final words and decided—no matter the magnitude of her fear, her impulse to run—she would be ready next time Someone came around.

Wren started dining alone in cafés, diners, bars, and restaurants just to be near other people, the movements and sounds of lives being lived together. On one of these solo excursions, Wren met a man in a yellow shirt who made her feel that the world was a good place, and the world was a good place because she was someone living in it.

From the moment they parted, Lewis left a gaping space in Wren's life. No one to feed. No one to check on. No one to drive to appointments. No one to love. No one to love her.

Wren went from gripping so totally to life to asking aloud *Why me?* to inanimate objects.

"Why me?" asked Wren of the Joshua trees and prickly pear cacti.

"Why me?" asked Wren of the stop signs.

"Why me?" asked Wren of jet streams.

"Why me?" asked Wren of cloudless skies.

"Why me?" asked Wren of the Chevron stations.

But, of course, nothing answered her question. Maybe she was not supposed to know.

After a day and a half on the road with only a few stops, Wren started to feel faint from hunger and fatigue. She pulled off at the first place she saw, a chain restaurant along a dry Arizona highway.

Wren sat at the bar, eating an amalgamation of deep-fried things, a meal her former self wouldn't have recognized as food at all. It seemed like everything she touched became dusted with sand, and with every bite, she felt its glassy grit between her teeth. She drank two beers faster than she should.

In the bathroom, she splashed water on her face, and a new woman appeared in the mirror, thin, tired, greasy, and alone. In the months since Lewis's diagnosis, she had changed alongside him. While caring for Lewis, Wren did little to decorate herself for the world. She'd gradually stopped doing her hair, makeup, and in recent weeks, even showering. Wren even got out of the habit of wearing her wedding ring because of the frequency with which she handled raw fish.

After one more beer, she found it easy to make conversation with strangers, like the truck driver named Tyler who told her his life story and all the sad things that had happened in it.

Wren watched his mouth move, speaking at her, for at least an hour. Tyler had perfect teeth, white and square. If he was devoted to his teeth, he is probably careful with other things, too. *Or maybe*, Wren thought, *he was simply obsessed with himself.* Whatever the reason, that night, Wren trusted teeth more than words.

When the bar closed, Wren followed Tyler to his rig, where he pressed her against his truck and kissed her. She dared herself to swipe her tongue across his teeth. They felt as smooth as they looked.

"It's been so long since I've talked to anyone,
especially a woman.
You're a good listener.
And you have kind eyes.
It's hard to find folks with kind eyes,

and trust me
I meet a lot of people on the road.
Most people,
they got all kinds of shiftiness in them,
but not you.
You're special.
You look at people direct.
And you're real pretty.
Not that slapped on kind of looking good
where everyone but the girl herself knows
she ain't hiding nothing.
. . .
Tell me something.
I hardly know a thing about you.
You know all about me.
It can be anything.
Do you live around here?"
"No, just passing through."
"Where to?"
"Dallas."
"Do you have a place to sleep tonight?" Tyler asked, massaging her
neck and shoulders with his thick hands.
"No."
"Well, you're more than welcome to stay. My truck sleeps two.
You don't have to if you don't wanna.
Wait.
Aren't you the actress, what's-her-name, from Texas?
The one in all those beauty pageant movies?"
"No."
"Are you sure?"
"Yes."

They laid snuggly together in his bunk behind the steering wheel of
his truck, and when Tyler offered her a beige oblong pill, she took it

unquestioningly. At first, she felt nothing at all, and then, half an hour later, her heart pulsed and swelled with false love and energy. She felt she could talk about anything, as if she'd known Tyler her whole life.

"My husband left me yesterday."

"Maybe he just needs his space.

Men need that, you know.

Independence and frontier."

"He said there were things he could not unsee."

"Any man who'd leave you is a goddamned-fool-piece-of-shit, I'll tell you that. Did I tell you my wife made this quilt we're laying on right now?"

"No."

"She made it without using a pattern or anything. She just cut the squares and sewed them all up together right on the kitchen table. Her hands had to touch every single part of it to make it. Miss her every day."

"How did she die?"

"She's not dead.

We're separated.

Well, divorced, actually.

I hate saying ex-wife. It just sounds *sad*.

I sometimes forget I'm not married to her."

"Too bad."

"I brought it on myself."

"What happened?"

"Didn't ever learn the difference between loneliness and being alone."

"So you cheated."

"Yup."

"In a hundred years,

we'll all be dead,

and then nothing will matter."

"What?"

"That's something my husband said once.

It gives you this immediate perspective.

Maybe life has no ceiling, no floors, no walls,

and we're free-falling from the moment we're born,

lying to each other,

agreeing to make invented ideas important,
to numb ourselves from the secret."

"What's the secret?"

"Maybe what happens between birth and death isn't as precious as we think."

"Come here, girl. Stop that sad thinkin'. Just come here," Tyler said, pulling her atop his chest. Then he started to laugh.

"What's funny?"

"It's just that
I've told you my entire life story,
but I forgot to tell you *Happy Thanksgiving*.
Happy Thanksgiving, little bird."

Wren closed her eyes, squinting tears out, and pretended Tyler was Lewis. Lewis's hands, Lewis's mouth, Lewis's hair, Lewis's neck, and the ceiling spun, spun, spun, spun, and her chest thumped, thumped, thumped, thumped. Then, just before dawn, she fell asleep in this strange man's arms, in this strange man's bed. But she was a stranger to herself, so what did it matter? They were two strangers holding each other for the night, and given the vast timeline of the universe, the difference between a night together and a lifetime seemed pretty much negligible.

She missed him so much.

Wren awoke, weighted by Tyler's hairy, heavy limbs. She was sweaty and nauseated, and the bunk was too small for her to move without waking him. Tyler tried to kiss her on the neck as she leaned away and reached for her shirt.

"Can I at least buy you breakfast before you go?"

"OK," Wren heard herself say. "I'm starving."

In the light of day, Tyler and Wren were awkward together. Tyler walked Wren to her car after a big diner breakfast before getting back on the road. Alone, Wren felt even hungrier than before she'd eaten.

She searched the glove compartment for a forgotten granola bar. Instead, she found a can of tuna she'd stashed for Lewis months ago. Wren pulled the tab on the can, gagged at the smell, and realized she didn't want food at all but rather, the feeling of emotional fullness, a hunger that could only be satiated by home, family, and familiarity.

If she stayed on the road, Wren could continue wrapping herself in the comfortable blanket of liminality. So she took a northern detour because returning home felt like a commitment to a life that could go on without him.

She took spontaneous turns on state highways through small towns. She ate dinners consisting of crackers and Coke. She stopped at rest areas to lie across picnic tables. She listened to happier travelers talk.

Will you walk the dog while I use the bathroom?

Take these chips away from me.

Only fourteen hours left until Vegas.

Give your brother his game back!

Over the next few days, Wren sent text messages Lewis would never read:

How strange it is to know someone—really know them. And then one day you realize you don't. Or maybe it is that I don't know myself.

There's a strong chance we will never see each other again. Unless you believe in spirits or the afterlife, which I don't.

Just pulled over to nap, and I had a dream you were still here. You had this goofy, awestruck look on your face, like maybe you'd just seen a double rainbow or a bobcat in the wild or a field of yellow blanket flowers, like the lot behind our house before they built the new subdivision. And I realized just now, after all this time, you were looking at me.

Back at the Grand Canyon, Wren climbed over the railing at the North Rim. The surface beneath her was uneven, a downward-facing wedge, daringly tilted.

The Grand Canyon looked different when she was by herself. With Lewis, all she saw were the depths of the ravines. Now she noticed the sky. No one really mentions the sky at the Grand Canyon, but the more she studied the situation, the more she thought the upward realm might really be the main event. The canyons would not be impressive if they weren't balanced by something infinitely vast.

Wren startled when a balding man with pants belted at the pudgiest part of his abdomen poked her shoulder.

"Sorry to bother you, ma'am, but would you mind taking our picture?"

"Sure," Wren answered reflexively.

In seconds, she had an expensive camera in her hand.

"You'll just press this button here and hold down this thing there, and when you see the red square, push the small black button twice, but not the small red button, never the small red button (that's for recording). And after you hold that button, keep the camera very still, press the larger black button till you hear the click."

"Okay," Wren said, camera in hand. "Say cheese."

"Cheeeeeeeese," echoed the family of four, and Wren instantly got the familiar hollow feeling. She hated this family, and at the same time, she wanted to be one of them.

"I took three," Wren said, handing over the man's camera. She could not bring herself to walk away.

"Maryanne, what do you think? Maybe for the Christmas card—except Jimmy is doing that weird thing with his shirt again," the man said to Maryanne as they reviewed the pictures. He felt Wren's lingering presence and interpreted it as her wanting something in return. "Oh! Do you want us to take a photo of you, miss?"

"No, thank you," Wren said. "I was just thinking that you have a beautiful family."

"That's so kind of you to say." Maryanne beamed.

Wren could not easily walk away now, because she had lingered past the point of invisibility. Her identity was crystallized to these people, and once she allowed herself to become solid to other human beings, she would be seen. After being seen, Wren risked being known, and being known came with the risk of loss. Even this small interaction cost her too much.

"Are you sure?" the man pressed.

"I'm traveling alone."

"Well, that's no excuse. We've got people to spare," Maryanne said, and Wren felt herself reaching into her back pocket for her phone and handing it over.

"Jimmy, Charlotte—*stop throwing rocks!* Be in a photo with this nice woman."

TEXT MESSAGES INTO THE ETHER

A couple dumb questions and an apology—

Why does my family always leave me?

Why am I so unlucky?

I'm sorry I didn't practice scuba diving more. I'm sorry I fell short. It should have been me, not you. Not you, who had so much to give the world.

Concentration wavering, Wren swerved into the centerline and grazed the ridges near the shoulder.

Utah tries so hard, she thought. Its geographical insecurity was so obvious: each big orange rock trying to outdo the one that came before it. Flamboyant, over-the-top features to disguise an otherwise arid and bereft landscape.

The first category of road people Wren noticed, The Clear Destination People, included weekend trippers, family vacationers, U-Haulers, and van-lifers, humming along with comfortable travel budgets in noble pursuits of self-exploration, hoping to leave behind the bad and discover an idealized version of themselves and even, life itself.

Wren belonged to the second category, The Wandering. Rest stops, fast food restaurants, and gas stations made up their territory. The Wandering were extras in The Clear Destination People's happier narratives, but The Wandering's anonymity was also advantageous. Wanderers did not have to be themselves. They could be no one.

As a new initiate, Wren saw the same types of people again and again. The chain-smoking man who squinted even when the sun wasn't bright. Grizzled truck drivers. Motorcycle guys. Middle-aged women pulling horse trailers behind battered pickups. Mousy young women with neon acrylic nails, meth mouth, and stick and poke tattoos, which made it easy to overlook the fact that they probably had mothers, grandmas, sisters, or aunts who were worried sick about them.

The Wandering recognized Wren as one of their own. They told her their stories, like the woman returning from her brother's memorial service in Palo Alto.

The woman could have been speaking to anyone or anything: a wall, sign, lamp, or dog. Wren was just what happened to be in front of her, pumping gas at the adjacent pump.

"My brother was so unhappy that he killed himself. Can you imagine doing that to yourself?"

"No," Wren lied. "How did he do it?"

"The bridge."

"*The* bridge?"

"Yes."

"Oh. Wow."

"He probably broke his neck as soon as he hit the water, which would have paralyzed him, and then he drowned. I hope he wasn't conscious. Do you think he was?" Dirty streams of tears and mascara made tracks down the woman's cheeks. Her pump clicked, and she replaced the handle, dripping gasoline all over her shoes.

"I don't know," Wren replied, this time telling the truth.

"I'd like to rent a boat to take out on Lake Powell. Do you have any available?" Wren asked over the phone when she was on the road again.

. . .

"Yes. For tonight."

. . .

"I'll be there by four o'clock."

Wren steered the houseboat into the sunset as if marching into a battle with night itself. When the marina was out of sight, she dropped anchor. She was freezing and found a blanket in the emergency kit behind the captain's seat. Drunk with exhaustion, Wren sat on the deck, wrapped herself in the blanket, and fell asleep, fatigue triumphing over cold.

An undetermined while later, Wren awoke shivering and startlingly displaced. In the nanosecond before she opened her eyes, she was once again within a life she knew and loved. Her life with Lewis before the diagnosis. Before doctors' appointments and dermal denticles and desperation. Before goodbye.

Lewis thought all children came into the world knowing some truth about magic and God. He thought the journey of adulthood was to forget about these things and then partake in the path to remembering. Lewis said one of the purposes of art was to point people toward what they already knew. Now Wren really needed to know: *Where is the art here, Lewis? And what path?*

Wren found a plastic canoe strapped to the exterior railing. She loosened the buckles, and the canoe plopped into the water just below the ladder. Without thinking, Wren lowered herself inside, found a weathered paddle, and began churning the water.

Wren's breath steamed the air ahead of her. Then she did the single thing you're not supposed to do in a canoe.

She stood up.

And not with the intent of maintaining balance, no. The canoe became a living entity with its own strategy. It rocked, swayed, and tilted. She wanted the shell of plastic to move her, determine her fate. Wren peered into the water. No wetsuit. No flippers. No oxygen tank. No order. No plan. No hiding. No mother. No husband.

Life is hard, she thought, and instantly reconsidered. *No. It is vicious.*

The canoe bucked her into the frigid lake.

Wren floated and then sank, the air leaving her body faster than it should. She did not fight for the surface. Instead, she surrendered to the lake's will. Sedated. Numb.

When she was a girl, she never swam in the middle of the lake by herself, fearing a garfish would mistake her for bottom sediments. Oh, the irony now; she'd just shared a bed, a house, a life with a great white shark for almost a year. Fish no longer frightened her. *Come for me,* Wren wanted to say. *I am all yours.*

She laughed. Or was it weeping? Maybe she was screaming. And then she felt the culmination of a life spent moving too quickly:

skinned knees
Father's Day
library books
thrift store sneakers
popular girls
SAT tests
Rachel
memorial arrangements
long days
anxious nights
shark's teeth
spreadsheets
promises kept
and broken
red dirt
orange skies
black oceans
pointless deserts
childhood lakes
hot winds
dying
denying
blistering
burning

seething
wringing
Lewis
Mom

"Stop."

She heard her mother's voice, which seemed to come through her body instead of from outside it. *Stop.* Wren thought she had forgotten her mother's voice, but how could she forget what had always been with her?

She felt her body relax, extremities tingling, and Wren saw her mother, Angela, as she was when Wren was ten years old.

"What are you doing here? *How* are you here?" Wren asked.

"Don't worry about that," Angela replied.

"Where am I?"

"You are safe."

"*Safe* isn't a real place."

"It is with me."

"Mom?"

"It's me," Angela replied.

"Is it *really* you?"

"It's really me."

While Angela floated before Wren, part human spirit and part sentient object, a glowing light surrounded Angela, and from this light, Lewis emerged, too.

He was dressed like he was going to work, but he had bare feet. Wren realized she forgot to say goodbye to his feet. She'd been so busy saying goodbye to the rest of him. They had the kind of conversation that's simultaneously of no and great importance:

LEWIS: Wren, you have your mother's chin!

WREN: I always thought I had her eyes.

LEWIS: No, those eyes belong to someone else. But you definitely have her chin.

WREN: This is a fascinating way for you to meet my mother.

ANGELA: Lewis is a lovely young man.

LEWIS: Thank you.

ANGELA: I'm so happy you found her. Wren is a lucky woman.

LEWIS: I am the lucky one.

ANGELA: Well, just so you know, Wren has her father's eyes.

WREN: All right, everyone.
    Let's please stop talking about eyes and feet and chins.
    I have a confession:
    I have been afraid my whole life.
    Mom, why was I the one responsible for remembering?
    I was just a girl.
    Sometimes I wish I could forget everything,
    even the good parts, and I'm sorry.
    And Lewis, I see it now, your unseeable place.
    It's so dark and empty.
    How could it have been here all this time and I never knew?
    . . .
    Hello?
    . . .
    Mom? Lewis?

They were both gone, dissolved by the water from which they came. Wren considered her options. She could follow Lewis and her mother into the void and revoke her tiresome flesh and blood experience. Or she could continue on in the world above. But for whom? And why?

Wren was so tired, so cold. Her body could sink no more. Rock bottom was the quietest, darkest place she'd ever been. She could no longer connect a thought to the one before it, and she genuinely wondered which one would be her last.

At Angela's memorial service, her mother's old friend George had told Wren what a strong and wonderful woman her mother was and how, in memory of Angela, who had been a very dear friend at one point in his youth, he wanted to be there for Wren. Any time, day or night, he'd be there for whatever she needed. Wren knew then this man with kind eyes and a silver-flecked hairline loved her mother very much. Maybe her mother loved him back. Now she needed George's help. Of all times, now. Wren had never prayed to anything in her life, but now she prayed to George. He was all she had left.

"Hello, George.

You may not remember me.

My name is Wren.

I'm Angela Wyatt's daughter.

We met at my mother's memorial?

I am praying to you because I'm in a bit of a bind.

I believe it is becoming rather urgent.

I believe I just hallucinated my late husband and mother, which was a lovely experience overall given the fact that they never met each other in real life, but it was also, in hindsight, a bit unsettling.

I believe myself to be a person of sound logic.

I believe myself to be a person with a firm handle on reality.

I also believe I am underwater.

I believe I could be drowning.

I do not believe in God, but I think I believe in you, George.

My husband wanted to make life more beautiful than when he found it so he could share it with the world:

friends

family

students

strangers

me.

But that was another life ago, and I'm sorry, George. I regret taking up your time this evening. I'm sure you have a nice family and things to do with them. Things better than listening to a drowning woman struggle with the past."

She waited for George to answer. He didn't. So Wren imagined him:

"You sound just like your mother," the Imagined George said.

"In which way? The timber of my voice? Or my choice of words? Or is it all of me? Are we just alike? I can't remember anything about her suddenly. My mother . . . Oh, yes! My mother could identify every bird by name, bake bread from scratch, and grow a garden in an eggshell."

"What's next for you?" the Imagined George asked in the winking but detached way of a good therapist.

"I might just stay right here."

The Imagined George laughed, perhaps acknowledging some familiar family neurosis.

"Imagined George, do you know what I think, do you? I think I've never known anything for sure."

Wren felt surprisingly warm, like she wasn't twenty feet deep in Lake Powell on the last day of November but in the middle of the most pleasant sunbeam: a tunnel of light hitting the houseboat on a spring morning, seeping through the windows, and waking her up with the sound promise of a greater heat to come. Wren was still alive, and she wanted to be.

Then she remembered robin's nests and rainbows and redbud trees and
long drives
big skies
soft, worn blankets
black-eyed Susans
hammock naps
treehouses
red-eared sliders
acorn wreaths
fairy rings
birthday crowns
cupcake dinners
honeysuckle
lake water
fried catfish

summer storms
moments of shared intuition
the autumn tree line at dusk
being enveloped by the warm C of a loving body
being the enveloper
being in the presence of Someone who believes you have something
worthwhile to say
being the one to whom important things are said
and bird wrists
and twig fingers
and strawberry moons
and finally: the symphony of hearts,
the internal music that plays when one decides to renew their
partnership with life.

Yet the symphony had been playing faintly all along, a barely discernible underscore amid the noise of her going, going, long-term-goaling, going, aiming, going, sweating, going, trying, going, failing, going, striving, going, working, going, going, hiding, going, going, moving, going, going, excelling, perfecting, succeeding, winning, compartmentalizing, going, going, going, going, going. But now the call toward life was loud, swelling, and triumphant—

like a brass section with one hundred instruments,
a musical theater ballad from a woman born to sing it,
or a rock band full of young and unknown geniuses.

Suddenly, with such insatiable yearning, Wren wanted to fill her lungs. She did not choose to be born, but she chose, in this moment, to live. So, by some power unbeknownst to her, her body rose to the surface of the lake, and when her head broke the surface,

shivering,
panting,
and blue,
she coughed,
took a breath,
and for the first time as one new and unborn once again—
She was open to the stars.

PART TWO

ANGELA

MAIN CHARACTERS

ANGELA: Wren's mother, an apologetic girl who will become a kaleido-scoping woman before our eyes—colorful, shape-shifting, drawn to the light.

MARCOS: Angela's boyfriend, a guy with ideas for hands and dreams for feet.

JULIA: Angela's friend, a portal to the good life.

GEORGE: Julia's brother, amateur herpetologist.

WREN: Angela's daughter, a logical child with exceptional stamina.

SETTING

Jefferson, Carter, and Love counties. Oklahoma. 1980–2005.

Without further ado—
Let us begin.
It is early summer.

Wren's mother, Angela, was a very nice girl. Perhaps one of the very few solidly nice girls left in the world. She cleaned up after herself and others without being told. She nodded and smiled to show she was listening. She gave compliments and brought cookies. She tested the temperature of a room before entering it. She apologized often, even if she did nothing wrong, just to be sure. Above all, Angela followed the rules, both spoken and unspoken, because within rules was order, inside order was peace, and within peace, she felt safe, even loved.

As an only child, Angela nurtured her parents, as if they were static fixtures in the house requiring regular maintenance. When her mother was upset, Angela told her she was beautiful and good. When her father was home on the weekend, Angela sat next to him while he watched *ABC's Wide World of Sports* so maybe he would not notice his wife crying or passed out on the trundle bed in the guest room from drinking too much.

SCENE: The Day Before Angela's Fifteenth Birthday

Angela sits at the kitchen counter eating cereal. Her mother, Colleen, enters from the other room.

COLLEEN: Happy sweet sixteen!

ANGELA: I'm turning fifteen. And not until tomorrow.

COLLEEN: You're looking mature for your age.

ANGELA: What do you mean?

COLLEEN: You don't want people to get the wrong idea about you. You're a good girl.

After Colleen went back upstairs, Angela remained frozen at the counter, watching her cornflakes become heavy, bloated rafts. She was not hungry anymore.

What did her mother mean by *people*? Did she mean *guys*? Because they noticed her every day. Guys noticed her everywhere she went.

For her fifteenth birthday, Angela wished for friends, so she wouldn't have to think so much about her parents' problems.

Angela often went days without seeing her father, and she suspected her mother did not see him much, either. He was gone when she woke up and did not come home until she was in bed.

Late at night Angela would hear the garage door beneath her bedroom window open and close. Clanging keys on the counter; cabinets opening and banging closed; plate clinking against knife; the hum of voices coming from the television. Angela tried to identify every auditory detail as if matching the sound to the activity would bring her father closer to her.

The summer and its solitude were the main ingredients contributing to the numbing boredom Angela came to expect when she didn't have school. Her limbs felt heavy, her thoughts were slow, and she was constantly sleepy even though she was not tired.

When she couldn't bear being home alone with her mother, who oscillated between needing Angela right by her side and wanting Angela out of her sight, she rode her bike to the always empty tennis courts at the country club.

With her mother's old racket, Angela served the tired tennis balls haphazardly across the net to no one.

When she got worn out from chasing balls, Angela lay faceup on the hot green concrete, pretending her body was a melting Popsicle. As she started to sweat, she imagined all the ugly parts of herself dripping away, leaving only her dream self, whom she deeply, truly, always wanted to be:

the girl with friends
the girl who was invited and included
the girl who went to parties and had plans
the girl who was never alone

One of these afternoons at the courts, a guy in a blue truck parked next to Angela's bicycle propped against the flagpole. A trail of black smoke from his exhaust pipe dissipated into the sky. The guy peeled off his sweaty T-shirt, flung it into his truck bed, and seconds later, swaggered through the gate with a racket in one hand and a canister of balls in the other. He was hairy all over and solid like a tree trunk. Angela tried not to stare. He was surely not a member of the country club.

Angela went to the tennis court every day at the same time, hoping to see the guy again. Just the thought of him gave her a feeling she had not experienced since she was a tiny girl who believed in Santa, each hour of December passing through a tunnel of strained, anticipatory patience.

The guy rolled up in his pickup again five days later, and when he stepped onto the court, it seemed all of nature—every leaf, blade of grass, dragonfly, sparrow, squirrel—turned to salute him.

Brown ridged stomach, glistening with bright beads of perspiration. Tan tree-trunk legs. Jet-black hair swooping around his movie-star jawline. Dunelike mounds of muscle on his chest and back. A satchel of tennis balls slung across a bulbous shoulder. Angela forgot how to breathe.

"Hey," the guy said, glancing Angela's way.

By the time Angela realized he'd spoken to her, it was too late to respond. The adjacent court felt like another country, and Angela did not have a passport.

Angela and the guy shared the court every afternoon for the next four days. During that time, Angela lost her mind.

She could not sleep, eat, or think about anything but the guy and his ridged stomach, tree-trunk legs, swoopy black hair, and the relief of muscles on his chest and back. She tried to imagine his smell, his story. She wondered if he thought of her. She wondered *what* he thought of her.

Every morning her first thought was of the guy. Would she see him again that day? And if she did, what would she say if he spoke to her?

On the fourth day, the guy looked right at her and winked. *(Winked!!!)*

"Have a good one," he said as he left, closing the gate behind him.

"**D**o you want to hit a few?" the guy asked on the fifth day.

"Okay," Angela squeaked, and a million angel trumpets sounded.

The guy held out his hand across the net for her to shake. His palm was rough and warm.

"Marcos," he said.

"It is nice to meet you, Marcos. My name is Angela," she somehow managed to reply.

Angela volleyed the ball into the other court every other minute and twice over the fence, but Marcos did not mind, because he loved instructing.

After tennis, Marcos invited Angela to his houseboat, where he lived on the lake. *Yes, that would be amazing,* she heard herself say. *I'd love to see your boat.* Angela felt like she might fly.

While they drove through town with Angela's bike in the truck bed, Marcos explained how he'd inherited the boat from his grandfather two years ago, fell in love with the idea of living on it, and somehow convinced the marina to create a job for him, Resident Boat Technician, even though he had never repaired a boat in his life.

"Wow. Amazing."

Angela could not stop saying *amazing*. As Marcos spoke, she tried to think of other words.

"I sell off parts of my boat in the summer, so I don't have to get a job in the off-season. Like yesterday, I sold the motor for a couple hundred bucks."

"That's . . . that's amazing," Angela replied.

Angela and Marcos had been sitting on the rooftop deck with their bare feet dangling since sunset, the conversation flowing so naturally that Angela forgot this was her same lonely life. She felt so comfortable around him.

"You ever been skinny-dipping?" Marcos asked around ten o'clock, when all the other boats turned off their lights.

"No, I haven't."

"Well, do you wanna?"

"What if people see us naked?"

"Then they see us."

Angela took off her sneakers, socks, shorts, and tank top inside the houseboat, folding them neatly and stacking them together, her heart pounding. She met a disrobed Marcos on the deck. Angela tried not to look at him.

"It's not real skinny-dipping if you've got your underwear on," he said.

Angela slowly, nervously took off the rest.

For a few seconds, Marcos and Angela stood together, naked in the moonlight. Marcos plunged first, gathering his knees in his arms and hitting the water like a cannonball.

"Angie, come on!" he bellowed from the water.

"Is it cold?"

"Jump!"

On a count of three, Angela stepped off the rooftop deck, holding her nose, straight as a toothpick.

That night, Angela crossed the invisible threshold separating childhood from the open plane of adult experiences. She jumped again and again and again, delighting in the second of free fall before the lake caught her. And Marcos was right. After a little warming up, she didn't care one bit if anyone saw her naked.

From here, things began to change for Angela in all the ways there were to change for a teenage girl over one summer.

She had overheard girls talk about it in hushed voices in the halls, after gym class, during lunch. Who had done it, who hadn't, if it hurt, if it hadn't, where, when, how, how much, and with whom. Now Angela did not understand their worries.

Sex was wonderful, and Angela had just found out she was quite good at it. Great, actually. She thought she might even be a natural expert. Marcos even told her so. His pet name for her was Overachiever because Angela had her first kiss and lost her virginity on the same night.

Funny, she wrote in the pink diary she secured with a heart-shaped lock and key, *how you get a kiss but lose your virginity. I don't feel like anything's been taken or added at all.*

Angela let Marcos fold her into his life until it seemed they had become one ingredient. She spent as much time with him as she could, and he seemed to want the very same thing. He was relaxed and sweet, experienced and strong. Angela didn't know it was possible to feel so nourished. He liked to talk, she liked to listen, and for a time, everything was perfect.

Marcos considered himself a spiritual man, and he believed his identification with spirituality was one of the things that made him special, wiser than everyone else, and exempt from adult responsibilities. To Marcos, God could appear in anything—the water, the sun, the fish, the weather. Even himself.

Before Marcos, Angela's concept of God did not extend past Easter Sunday and Christmas. On these occasions, Angela would stand between her parents in the pew wearing a frilly, stiff dress from Sears. Her father held the hymnal but never sang. Her mother's insecure eyes darted around the room, calculating and cataloging who's who in her head.

"I'd like for us to go to church more often," Angela's father said in the car after the Easter Sunday service a few years before.

"Maybe I'd go to church more if I thought Jesus was the kind of man who could handle a little criticism," her mother replied, passive-aggressive.

"Well, he could handle being *crucified*," Angela's father muttered. He understood a bit more about Jesus than his wife thought.

Then Angela's mother rolled her eyes and said something to the effect that nothing could save her. Nothing could save anyone. Not even Jesus, which was probably why she drank.

Angela fell in love with Marcos's pain, because it was quite like her own. They were both neglected by their mothers, unknown to their fathers, and ill at ease with people their own age.

"Angie, you and me, we're loners because we're special," Marcos said one morning as they snuggled together in the sleeping cabin. "No matter how you skin it, each other is all we got."

When Angela first started staying the night with Marcos, she told her mother she was having a sleepover with a new, invented friend, Lisa. This one-time explanation extended to every night she was away, and neither of her parents worried about her increasing absence at home.

Angela returned every few days to raid the housekeeper-stocked pantry, gather clean clothes, and make sure her mother was still breathing. During these visits, her mother would ask about Lisa, attempting to contact life through the fog. But she did not listen for the answer, so Angela never gave a substantive one.

Angela's father did not require excuses, because he didn't notice if she slept at home or not. It was his wife's role to keep track of the child and his to provide for it.

It seemed that Angela's absence made no difference to her family, but her presence meant very much to Marcos. And in his company, unlike at home, Angela was never bored.

In a single day, Marcos would sleep until noon, meditate, draw, read, practice diving off the rooftop deck, go noodling for catfish, replace someone's dead boat battery, swim to the tower and back, make friends with campers who would invite them to cookouts, and after sundown, captivate the entire campground, making up songs and ghost stories on the fly. Marcos could make anything seem true.

From the moment Angela met Marcos, time became irrelevant and strange. A day together felt like an epic novel, an unending adventure story, and a moment without him seemed gray and slow. Talking to anyone but him was like trying to speak with a mouthful of molasses, and Angela realized her whole life had been molasses.

Most important of all, Marcos was the first person who'd ever valued Angela and treated her thoughts and feelings with care, and when Angela saw herself through his eyes, she began to see all of life optimistically.

He said such nice things, the most wonderful things anyone had ever said to her. She tried to memorize his sentences the moment they were spoken so she could relive and admire them later. While walking through the woods by herself, Angela repeated Marcos's words like mantras. With each utterance, Angela felt herself minutely changing, finally becoming the girl she had always wanted to be:

    the girl with friends

    the girl who was invited and included

    the girl who went to parties and had plans

    the girl who was never alone

    the girl who was loved

SPECIAL WORDS

"I love knowing what you think," Marcos said as they hiked around the lake, and Angela was so happy she felt she might float away.

"I'm proud of you," Marcos said often and out of the blue, even when Angela felt she'd done nothing at all.

"You can ask me for help," he said, looking her in the eyes so she would know he meant it.

"Well, hey there, Overachiever," Marcos said, kissing her on the cheek as she climbed into the passenger seat. "Looks like the fun just arrived."

The day after the Fourth of July, Marcos combed the man-made beach by the campgrounds for coins and lost jewelry with a metal detector he "borrowed" from the back of a stranger's pickup over the weekend. He'd found an engagement ring once, just an inch deep in the sand, and ever since then, the beach had offered the endless potential for riches.

Meanwhile, Angela had something big on her mind. That morning, the cashier at the Bait 'N Tackle Shop called Marcos her *boyfriend*. They had never discussed being girlfriend and boyfriend, and Angela had not previously thought about giving their relationship a title, but now she urgently needed to know.

"Marcos," Angela began, nervous, as he waved the detector across a patch of sand. "I'm sorry, but am I your girlfriend?"

"What?" asked Marcos, confused and a bit frightened.

"Am I your girlfriend?"

"I need to go see my weed guy in Thackerville," Marcos announced.

Angela followed him to his truck, expecting to accompany him like always, but instead, he pushed the metal detector into her arms. "Take this. Stay here."

"When will you be back?" Angela asked as he started the engine.

"Don't know," Marcos replied before doing a donut in the empty gravel lot and driving off.

After Marcos left, Angela borrowed a neighboring church camp's kayak to explore one of the shallow coves. The swampy water contained a small universe: fish, toads, tadpoles, mayflies, algae-coated life vests, beer cans, and deflated water toys.

Then, as she paddled through cattails, Angela's silver charm bracelet slipped off her wrist. She had not taken it off since her mother gave it to her three years earlier. Angela had just turned twelve, the year her mother stopped drinking for eight months. When her mother gave her the bracelet, she said Angela could pick out a new charm on every special occasion. But her mother would neglect the charm bracelet, like she did most things. And Angela continued to wear it as a reminder of the promise that things might one day be better because they had been, once before.

Before, before, before, before. What came before? At once, sitting alone in a borrowed boat covered in new mosquito bites, Angela could not remember *before*.

She scrambled out of the kayak and searched the murky water. She fished through fistfuls of mud, looking and hoping for three hours. Just before sunset, a cloud cloaked the lake in its shadow, and Angela heard thunder in the distance. Paddling in, she tried to accept the sad news. It was gone.

Angela found seven leeches on her calves after she returned the kayak and tried not to cry as she peeled them off. But Angela wasn't crying about the leeches. Along with the bracelet, she felt she'd lost part of herself. The part that used to make paper dolls. The part that bicycled to the courts by herself. The part that remained in her parents' house in the lonely bedroom above the garage. The part of her that was still innocent, a virgin, somebody's little girl.

Marcos returned at dusk, too high to notice Angela's puffy, red face. Angela got high herself for the first time that night, lying atop the roof deck. Within a few minutes, she had the most terrible feeling.

The crackling radio in the distance, the june bugs clinking their pill bodies into the light overhead, and Marcos's unremitting chatter suddenly felt deafening and unbearable. A bolt of tension radiated from the middle of her chest. Her throat tightened; she struggled to breathe; she thought she was dying. In contrast, Marcos seemed unequivocally at peace, with his hands laced across his chest and thumbs tapping to some internal melody.

"Hey, Marcos?"

"Yep."

"Am I alone?"

"Yes, but we all are, when you think about it."

The same night, a big storm rocked the boat inside the stall. Marcos got out of bed to secure the boat with more ropes, and when he came back, Angela stood at the door, face white as the moon.

"What's wrong, baby?"

"Marcos, I'm sorry, but will you please take me home?"

SCENE: Thunderhead

We hear Angela's mother, Colleen, before she enters Angela's bedroom, wearing poorly attached fake eyelashes and the Hawaiian-print muumuu she wore over her bathing suit when they used to vacation in Florida. Colleen exclaims in profanity (brief improvisation) after stubbing her toe on Angela's dresser.

COLLEEN: Did you know your father lost his patients? His practice?

ANGELA *(groggy)*: Mom?

COLLEEN: He just stopped showing up to work. *Six months ago! What on God's green earth?* Haven't you heard that story before? This is just like a goddamned movie. All men are the same. I should have left ten years ago. No—I should have never married him in the first place. I hate this house.

ANGELA: Mom, go to bed. You're drunk.

COLLEEN: Oh, no, sweetie...

ANGELA: You need to rest.

COLLEEN: I'm a terrible mother. You didn't need to hear... I'm sorry, sweetie. Am I a terrible mother?

ANGELA: You're a very good mother.

Colleen sits at the end of Angela's bed.

COLLEEN: Tell me things about your life. I want to know everything. What's new?

ANGELA: Nothing.

COLLEEN: There must be something. How is your friend? Lisa, isn't it?

ANGELA: She is fine.

COLLEEN: I bet you can think of one thing. One new thing to tell your mom.

. . .

ANGELA: Okay . . .
    Well,
    there is this one thing.
    I don't know.
    Maybe it's not a big thing.
    It feels like a big thing,
    but it could be nothing.
    Have you ever looked at the world in a new way, like, it's the same world you've always seen, but now it's different in a very important way, and you can never look at it in the old way ever again? And you want to look at it in the old way, but you know the new way is better, sort of?
    I've never done this before.
    Or felt this way.
    It's weird.
    I don't know.

It's dumb.
I'm dumb.

COLLEEN: I'm sure it's not dumb.

ANGELA: Well, I think I'm in love with somebody.

COLLEEN: Oh, baby. Who is it?

. . .

ANGELA: A boy from school. He was in my social studies class.

COLLEEN: Have you told him how you feel?

ANGELA: No.

. . .

COLLEEN: Can I hold you again, like when you were little?

Of course, Marcos was the very opposite of anyone who was in Angela's social studies class.

He thought dreams were messages from ghosts and spirits, and although Angela privately found this idea a bit preposterous, she still fabricated dreams because she knew it would please him. Yet, amid the pressure of wanting to produce rich dreams for Marcos to analyze, Angela started having them.

"Last night, I dreamed I was the stem of a pear," Angela told him excitedly as they feasted on their standard meal, peanut butter and Wonder bread, both of which she'd taken from her parents' house.

"A seedling metaphor, interesting."

"My arms were leaves that were also wings. I thought I could fly, but every time I tried, I found myself stuck to the pear, which made me way too heavy for flying. Then a gust of wind tipped me over, and I cried out for help, but no one was there to put me right side up. And then I woke up."

The first crisp day in September felt like a legitimate miracle, and the bathwater lake got cooler day by day. By the end of October, the boat at night felt like the inside of a refrigerator.

To distract themselves from the chill, Marcos and Angela filled the cabin with marijuana and cigarette smoke, which gave her thoughts the quality of warm taffy, expanding and condensing in long, heavy minutes.

Angela always had math homework, reading for English Literature, or the threat of a history pop quiz, but when she was with Marcos, she had trouble focusing on anything she had to do.

Angela became mesmerized by the water rolling down her fuller breasts, hips, and stomach in the shower. She considered these changes, at first, to be the final branch of puberty. By her third missed period, however, Angela knew what she had to know. She was naive in many ways, but there was no denying this.

Angela rode her bike to Sonic after school on a Friday and then to the park behind the Baptist Church. She drank a cherry limeade so fast she forgot to taste it. Lying beneath a cypress tree, she welcomed her baby telepathically, telling it all about herself and the world:

"Hello.

I suppose we should get to know each other now.

I grew up in a big house about four miles from here,

give or take.

My mother, well . . .

I'd rather not describe her.

But my dad is a doctor.

Well, was. I think.

These are your grandparents.

As for your dad—

you will meet him soon.

And me, I am your mother.

How nice to say.

My other name is Angela,

but you may call me anything you like.

(As long as it's nice.)

I'm sure I will like anything you think of."

Angela put a hand on her belly and another on her heart and said aloud for the second time in a year: "I think I'm in love with somebody."

Angela managed to contain the news until they were fishing for their supper at dusk, standing at the end of the pier.

"I have news," she began.

"Yeah?" Marcos replied, his eyes on the bobber.

"I'm having a baby."

Marcos lowered his fishing pole and took a step backward. Angela couldn't tell if he was going to run away or embrace her.

An entire history passed through Marcos's mind: watching his papa put on a suit on a 90-degree day to sell used cars; sitting shoulder to shoulder on the hood of Papa's truck, shooting Coke cans with a BB gun; waiting in deer stands for hours in the fall; smelling his cheap cologne at church, an inadequate mask for the previous night's liquor; being carried on the shoulders of a hero, his papa before prison, feeling one hundred feet tall.

"Are you sure?" Marcos asked after an extended silence.

"Yeah."

"Very sure?"

"Yeah, I think so."

"Well, then. We'll be a family here."

"Really?"

"That's what I said."

Marcos dotted kisses from Angela's forehead to her navel. Standing on his knees, he rested his cheek on her stomach and wrapped his arms around her thighs, momentarily a small boy hanging on to his mother's dress, his only sanctuary from the world.

They said the word *family* back and forth until it lost its meaning and felt like gush in their mouths. Angela was happy, but beneath the joy, she felt intuition's soft pull reminding her:

Nothing bad lasts forever.
Neither does anything good.

SCENE: Family Meeting

Angela sits across the kitchen table from her parents. They are eating an array of classic American breakfast foods. The low buzz of the refrigerator underscores the tension. The light from the window above the sink casts a spotlight on Angela.

Rick keeps clearing his throat as he spreads strawberry jelly on three pieces of toast.

Angela takes a small bite of scrambled eggs. She feels nauseated this morning.

Colleen fidgets with her wedding ring, the only part of her marriage that touched her to the point of knowing.

RICK: I'm sure you've noticed things have been strained in our home the past few months.

COLLEEN: Years.

RICK: A long time. Things have been hard for a long time.

COLLEEN: Yes.

Colleen and Rick look at each other, deciding who should step off the cliff first.

221

COLLEEN: And that's why your father and I have decided to divorce.

ANGELA: Oh.

COLLEEN: You're going to stay here with your father, and I'm going to take a little trip and find somewhere else to live. We know this is a big change, but it doesn't change that your father and I love you very much.

RICK: Do you have any questions?

ANGELA: I actually have news of my own.

COLLEEN: What is it, sweetie?

ANGELA: I'm having a baby.

RICK: Jesus H. Christ.

COLLEEN: Oh no, honey. Are you sure?

ANGELA: I'm sure. And really, it's fine. It's good news.

RICK: You're thirteen years old!

COLLEEN: She's sixteen.   ANGELA: I'm fifteen.

RICK: Who is he?

Angela starts to glow faintly and then stronger as the scene around her dims.

ANGELA: He's very special.
    He can take apart an engine, put it back together again,
    and sometimes it works better than it did when it was brand-new.
    He lives on a houseboat and wakes up at five a.m.
    to swim

write poetry
or paint the sunrise
because it inspires him.
And there's this way he sees things,
like yesterday, we were looking out at the lake, and he noticed a tiny
turtle swimming through the water.

RICK: Angela, who is—

ANGELA: And Marcos said, "Look here, Angie.
    The turtle may venture into the land a few feet
    or sit on a rock
    but for the most part,
    for this turtle,
    it's just the lake."
    And how much exists outside of the lake that the little turtle will
    never know!
    There are oceans, cities, and continents!
    And think about it, Mom and Dad:
    We're just like that little turtle.

COLLEEN: You'll have to go away to have the baby. Or marry him.

ANGELA: I am not going away. Marcos said I could live with him. And
he doesn't believe in marriage, and to be honest, I don't, either.

Rick inhales to remark but realizes, especially given the previous announce-ment, he has nothing left to say.

On the eve of the previous scene, the Family Meeting, Rick tugged at the soft flesh of Colleen's inner elbow for the first time in over two thousand days. With the tenderness of an introverted adolescent boy, he asked, *Would you like to sleep in my room tonight?* Colleen declined.

He was very surprised to see Colleen beside him the next morning, hair tossed and tangled with an arm hanging off the side of the bed, the same as always.

Rick could handle the sight of an open wound, work for twenty hours with no sleep, and tell a patient they were dying, but he did not have the courage to hold his own wife, tell her she needed help, or say he would love her until the day he died. Yes, he was a man of his era, one in a generation of boys who were trained to lead but never feel, one in a generation of boys who became staunch, withholding men in lonely rooms, looking out at life with no way to touch it.

Rick pretended to be asleep until his soon-to-be-ex-wife got up to prepare a final breakfast for their disbanding family of three.

In the following days, Colleen prepared the Volkswagen and pranced around the house, preemptively thrilled to travel, to live, to love, to explore, to breathe—*to find myself!*

Colleen thought of her trip as an adventure, picking up where she left off at age seventeen, the year she got married.

Rick thought of the days ahead, alone in his big house, as hell on earth.

Angela wasn't old enough to get a driver's license, buy cigarettes, or vote, but she was the perfect age to worship the first guy who said she was important. And even though she was still a child herself, she could, at only fifteen, live on his boat and have his baby.

So, this is what it feels like to love your life, Angela thought often.

The next month would be one of the happiest times of Angela's life so far. Unlike puberty, pregnancy was a physical transition with a tangible end. Angela had no precept for motherhood, but she felt very confident about her ability to do a great job. She found herself skipping and smiling all the time for no reason at all.

The thought of her parents once evoked an involuntary ache in her chest, but now she experienced a new uncaring neutrality. Angela's future felt so full, and her parents existed another life ago, ghosts relieved from the duty of haunting.

When Marcos said he was "almost broke," it was not hyperbole, a veiled accusation, or an abstraction, the fear of not having money, as Angela's father meant it. Despite their dwindling resources, Marcos said he was not worried. He said he did not think about money on principle. What the principle was, Angela was not sure. But to that end, she did not think about money much, either.

Marcos did not like it when Angela went to her parents' house anymore, even if it was just to gather food. He said he did not trust her father.

When they spent the last five bucks and there were no boat parts left to sell, Marcos got a job at the tire factory, begrudgingly shelving his maverick identity. He worked the second shift and got home after eleven o'clock at night smelling of vulcanized rubber, machine oil, and cigarette smoke.

Thanks to a premature ice storm and the convenient failure of the heating system at the high school, Angela wore her coat indoors all day long. For a while, no one at school could tell she was pregnant.

But overnight, it seemed, Angela had nothing to wear. Her jeans wouldn't rise above her knees, and it was too cold for skirts or dresses.

Soon everyone knew Angela's name and what was happening to her. They couldn't kick a girl out of high school for being pregnant, but they could certainly drill a hole through her spirit.

Angela dropped out. Even if she hadn't been pregnant, there were kinder environments to exist in than tenth grade.

For instance: a decent library book, the hike to Buzzard's Roost in the middle of a weekday, or Sunday evening, no longer the pinnacle of dread. Even tempering Marcos's moodiness and growing unrest about impending fatherhood was leaps better than any day of high school.

Yet spending so much time on the boat forced Angela to notice things she had not seen before in Marcos. He could be mean, rolling his eyes if Angela asked him to do one small thing. He stole from people constantly and without hesitation. He never told Angela where he was going or when he would return, sometimes disappearing for days at a time. Most upsetting of all, the more visibly pregnant Angela became, the more invisible and uninteresting she was to him, no matter what she said or did.

SCENE: A Boy and a Woman

Angela finds Marcos at the end of the pier, drawing the barren trees reflecting on the surface of the lake

ANGELA: I like your picture. I've never seen you draw trees that way.

MARCOS: Would you sit, please? Or leave? You're messing with the light.

Angela sits.

ANGELA: Hey, Marcos?

MARCOS: What?

ANGELA: I'm sorry, but lately,
    I've felt so lonely.
    Are you angry with me?

Marcos slaps his pencil down, and it falls between a crack in the planks and into the lake.

MARCOS: Dammit!

ANGELA: I'm sorry.

MARCOS: Is that all you had to say?

ANGELA: I'm sorry, but I just miss how it used to be.

MARCOS: Maybe I'm exhausted from working so *you* can have a nice life.

ANGELA: I could work, too.

MARCOS: What did you say?

ANGELA: I said I could work, like you.

MARCOS: Nothing is ever enough for you.

ANGELA: I didn't mean that at all. I'm sorry.

Marcos grabs her face with his hand and brings her face close to his.

Angela's jaw is a branch he can snap in half in his young, strong hands.

Then Marcos recognizes Angela's eyes, holding the urgency and fear of a hunted animal right before it gets put out of its misery, before the boom, before it all goes dark.

She knew it was wrong to think this way, but seeing Marcos's mulberry thumbprint beneath the soft flap of her earlobe the next morning gave Angela the creeping satisfaction that he took the time to touch her.

"I thought about what we talked about," Marcos said with a mouthful of peanut butter and bread. "You should find a job."

"Okay, I will."

"Well, what are you waiting for?"

Angela put on her only outfit that still fit and went over to the Bait 'N Tackle Shop to ask if they needed anyone else to work the cash register.

They weren't hiring. Same for the gas station at the marina.

Angela walked a mile or so down the road to her only other prospect, the Cross Timbers Motel.

"May I please speak to your manager?" Angela asked the woman at the front desk, whose name tag read Patricia.

"I'm the manager."

"I'm looking for work. Are you hiring?"

A little while later, Angela sat on a bench outside with Patricia, who smoked while she conducted Angela's interview.

"Are you a tidy person?"

"Yes."

"Describe your ability to work with others."

"Good, I think."

"Are you able to lift thirty pounds?"

"I think so."

"Will you show up on time?"

"Yes."

"Felonies?"

"No."

"High school diploma?"

"No."

"When is your baby due?"

"March, I think."

"We don't allow babies or kids at work."

"I understand."

This girl looks like a disaster, but I like her, thought Patricia. She had a soft spot for people she thought she could help.

"What is your name?"

"Angela."

"All right, Angela. Come tomorrow morning, 'round seven. Julia will train you on linens."

Angela's job was to launder all the hotel linens alongside Julia, who could convincingly be any age between sixteen and twenty-five. She had the most beautiful hair Angela had ever seen in real life, black and shiny like satin. Angela restrained herself from reaching out to touch it. Also, Julia was tall, which was important because they needed to stack the towels up to the ceiling.

Julia contained all her length in a quiet, sustained elegance. Even her fingers were interesting to watch. As she explained how the machines worked and the different kinds of towels the motel used, her movements looked like a choreographed dance.

First they separated the towels from the sheets and pillowcases. Before starting a laundry load, Julia added the chemicals, detergent and bleach, to the machine. When the cycle was done, Angela loaded the damp linens into the dryer while Julia started the next load. They both folded during the cycles, and when they ran out of things to do, Julia read a magazine and Angela, a book left by a motel guest on the nightstand.

They worked in tandem six days a week, and each day, Angela tried to spark a friendship. It had been so long since she'd spent time with anyone who wasn't Marcos. A few attempts:

Would you like to sit and fold for a while, Julia? I don't need the chair.
What part of town do you live in?
Do you like books?
I like your braid.
I miss school, especially the library.
Julia was slow to warm.

It wasn't Julia's nature to be friendly and outgoing, but Angela learned she was brave and true when it mattered:

"See her? That is what a bad girl looks like," a woman whispered loudly to her preadolescent daughter, pointing at Angela as they passed the cleaning cart in the hall.

Without a moment of hesitation, Julia charged up to the woman, stopping only a few inches from her face.

"Don't talk that way about my friend. You know nothing about her," Julia hissed, and the woman shepherded her daughter away, guilty.

"You didn't have to do that," Angela whispered when Julia returned.

"Hell yeah I did," Julia said. "That lady's an idiot. She doesn't know the first thing about you."

An uncomplicated friendship began to emerge.

Julia revealed she did not want to work at the motel forever. She would love to be a nurse if she didn't hate school so much. Ever since her girlhood friends turned on her in junior high, Julia had mistrusted women. She said her twin brother, George, was her best friend. Julia's family was Chickasaw, and no one left home unless they were in trouble with the law or crossed someone in a bad way.

Some days they were silent, and other times they talked all day.

Julia brought Angela food: bricks of homemade cornbread, jars of blackberry jam, and foil-wrapped bundles of smoked pork. "From my mom," she would say.

If their shifts ended at suppertime, Julia would invite Angela to eat with her family, and George would pick them up from the motel.

Julia's family was like her: unpretentious, only functionally polite, bold yet unobtrusive, and most of all, genuine.

Theresa, Julia's mother, made Angela take home all the extra food. The first time, Angela tried to refuse it, but Theresa stared her down with such concentration and seriousness that Angela didn't dare refuse an offering again.

At least a dozen circulating regulars came and went regularly, dropping off bags of potatoes, seeds, rice, hamburger meat, diapers, or dog food—not in exchange for the family's hospitality but as a contribution to that which belonged to all of them. Unlike Angela's childhood home, which was full of unused pretty things, everything at Julia's house had a purpose.

The entire extended family lived in a cluster of trailer homes on three hundred twenty acres along the Red River. Generations of them were buried just fifty yards from the house. They had chickens, horses, and cattle, grew a few vegetables, and shared their space so thoroughly that instead of five individual trailer homes, it felt like one big house. Angela grew up in a small town just thirty miles east on Highway 70, but Julia's life in the country seemed like an entirely different world.

At any given moment, four or more people were yelling, talking, laughing, crying, eating, or sleeping. There were always too many people for the space indoors, so conversations and suppers spilled outside on the grass.

No one among Julia's family or friends passed judgment on Angela, the only white girl in the group. But a few, especially Theresa, worried.

Theresa watched Angela interact with her daughter, and it was so obvious that Angela lacked a critical toughness for what lay ahead as a very young mother. Theresa also had a baby at fifteen, but unlike Angela, she had a community of mothers surrounding and supporting her.

Angela is a sweet girl, and I will do my best to help her, Theresa thought as she gave Angela second helpings of beans, rice, and cornbread. *But there are bruises on her arms.*

October concluded the "buggy months," what Julia referred to as the time between April and October when a variety of biting and blood-sucking insects made the prospect of walking through the tall grass quite unappealing.

November, however, brought a new menu of activities. George would lead the way across the family's vast acreage with a rifle hanging on his shoulder, not because he was hunting anything but for self-defense if they encountered a rabid coyote, skunk, or mountain lion.

Julia and George knew the land as well as they knew each other. Every creek, spring, grove, hill, and ridge had a story. In these stories, the boundaries between the living and dead became thin if not completely transparent. Angela began to understand why people in Julia's family rarely moved away. The family's lives and the land were bound to each other as if they were the same body.

During those exploratory afternoons, Angela learned George had a passion for snakes and preferred native Oklahoma snakes to "the more popular snakes" (a phrase that both horrified Angela and made her laugh), especially copperheads, water moccasins, black rat snakes, and diamondbacks.

George was tall, like his sister. To talk to him, Angela tilted her head up and made her hands into a megaphone, or George hunched down, hands on knees, to hear her. (This began as a joke about their height difference, but then they both began to earnestly appreciate its practical application.)

George usually smiled with his mouth closed (probably because his teeth were grievously crooked). But if a joke caught him off guard, he might forget to hide, liberating both overlapping teeth and electric joy. All Angela wanted to do was beam back at him, maybe forever.

Angela, Julia, and George all got Thanksgiving off, so the three of them trekked down to the Red River's broad white beach in the morning. The river was not precisely red but rather a deep rust. George collected driftwood and built a fire on the beach while Julia and Angela skipped rocks across the river's glassy surface.

Walking back to the house through the middle of an open pasture, Angela sensed a benevolent presence, an embracing, silent witness.

"I always feel so good out here. It's hard to describe," Angela said.

"Oh, that's a God thing," Julia replied as if this were an obvious fact, like gravity.

"Julia's smiling so much now," Theresa said, mostly to herself, while George helped her with the dishes after the Thanksgiving meal.

"Yeah, she seems really happy," George replied, and he was happy, too.

Even though it felt wrong to do so, George thought very often:

I think I like that girl.

I like her a lot.

On Christmas Eve morning, Marcos ate a few magic mushrooms and wandered into the woods.

Angela imagined how the evening would go if Marcos returned from his trip in a wonderful mood. She would ask him to come with her to Julia's for Christmas Eve; he might exclaim *Yes!,* embrace her, kiss her big belly.

At a quarter to four o'clock, Angela spotted Marcos swimming toward the boat from across the lake. (He still swam for exercise as if it were July.)

"Hey!" Angela called out.

"What?" Marcos hollered back, his head bobbing in the water.

"I have something to ask you."

"CAN'T HEAR YOU."

"I'M GOING TO JULIA'S FOR CHRISTMAS EVE. DO YOU WANT TO COME?"

"WHO IS THAT?"

"MY FRIEND. THE ONE I TOLD YOU ABOUT. FROM WORK."

"I DO NOT SUPPORT THE CAPITALIST CONSTRUCTION OF JESUS CHRIST. YOU KNOW THIS."

Then Marcos dipped his head under, like a snapping turtle that had just come up for air, and continued his cold swim.

Angela did not have time to feel disappointed, because five minutes later, George and Julia arrived to pick her up for supper.

C ars lined the shoulder of the road for a hundred yards in either direction of the family compound. There weren't enough seats for everyone indoors, so Angela and Julia sat in George's truck bed wrapped in Julia's bedspread for warmth and devoured plates of ham, sweet potato casserole, cornbread, and gravy.

After pie, some cousins set off fireworks in the pasture, and the families with young children went home. The remaining teenagers and adults sat around the firepit, a circle of boulders arranged around a smaller circle of rocks which held a crackling fire. George failed at the same card trick three times, and everyone tried not to laugh. When he failed the fourth time, no one could keep it together.

"I could do the trick this afternoon. I swear. I did it ten times!" George exclaimed.

Julia went inside to help her aunts pack leftovers. The cousins left to find more firewood. Angela and everyone else watched three dogs with zoomies playfully antagonize one another in the yard.

"Hey, Angela," George whispered, startling her.

"What?"

"Can I show you something?"

"Depends. What kind of thing are you thinking?"

"Don't be so suspicious. It's something amazing."

"Well, okay."

Then George took Angela's hand, and he led her as if they were two kids entering an imaginary world, into the darkness beyond the floodlights, the coyotes sounding nearer and nearer.

"Aren't you scared?" Angela asked.

"Nah. Are you?"

"A little."

"They ain't gonna bother us."

"How do you know?"

"Just know," George replied.

George and Angela hiked across the night prairie until they reached the highest point, a vista that saw all the way to Texas on a clear day.

"You can see all the constellations up here," George said. "What do you think?"

"It's . . ."

Angela's mind filled with a million thoughts and then none. Even though she was seven months pregnant, her body felt limp and light, as if each pinprick of gleaming starlight were gently reeling her up to live among them. Beneath this great, glittering dome of stars and shard of new moon, Angela got the feeling, somehow, that she might belong to everything and everything to her.

". . . so beautiful," she finished. George understood.

When they returned, Julia had already gone to bed. Angela could not stop yawning.

"Can I take you home?" George asked.

"That'd be nice. Thank you," Angela replied.

George drove like Angela was made of porcelain, slowing over potholes and stopping completely at every stop sign even though the roads were always quiet that time of night.

"You ever seen a couple hundred diamondbacks wrigglin' around in the same bucket?" George asked out of nowhere.

"No," replied Angela, suppressing her laughter. "It had better be a pretty big bucket."

"I'm gonna take you to the Waurika Rattlesnake Hunt next year. You've never seen more diamondbacks in your life."

"Okay . . ."

"Now, don't make that face! You're gonna love it. I know you're gonna love it."

All the lights flipped on inside the boat when they arrived at the marina, and Marcos stepped out on the deck, watching them. Immediately, Angela knew something was wrong. She swallowed hard as George ran around to open her door. Angela held his hand as she stepped down onto the gravel.

"Merry Christmas, Angela," George said, feeling warm all over even though he forgot his jacket.

"Merry Christmas to you, too, George."

George replayed their conversation about the Rattlesnake Hunt, recalling the way Angela had fidgeted with the buttons on her coat and how, when he'd held out his hand, she'd grabbed it tight. It seemed Angela did not want to let go.

And George—well, he did not want to let her.

"Where were you?" Marcos demanded, pushing her against the countertop. Angela winced. His breath and sweat smelled just like her mother's.

"I told you. I was with my friend," Angela said.

Marcos drilled into her as if eye contact were a reliable means to determine the truth.

"You need to be resting, prioritizing the family. Not staying out late."

"I'm sorry."

"I want you to quit going to that job and seeing those people."

"I thought we needed money," Angela said.

"For Christ's sake, Angela, let me be *a man*."

"But you said . . ."

"You're not listening to me, Angie."

Angela's body clenched as he moved in to kiss her neck. He combed his rough hands through her hair.

"You smell like smoke."

"There was a campfire."

"I miss how things used to be," Marcos said, his voice creating steam inside her ear. He unhooked her bra. "You promise you'll stop going over there?"

"I promise." Angela tried to pull away, but Marcos grabbed her wrist.

"You promise, promise?" Marcos whispered, pressing himself into her.

"Promise, promise," Angela uttered.

"Do you love me?"

Then Angela's mind left her body, and she tried to return to the stars. Why didn't she go with them, gleaming, when they called her to join them in the dome of bright sky? And where was God now? Was there anyone out there, anything real, who could protect her now?

Angela gave her notice at the Cross Timbers, telling everyone she was quitting because of the baby.

"You come right back when you're ready," Patricia said. "You hear?" Outside of being worried about her, Patricia saw Angela's potential. She loved to learn and made everyone around her better.

On Angela's last day, she and Julia worked together as usual, the synchronized dance with four hands. Patricia turned on the No Vacancy sign outside for the first time in two years, because of the high school basketball tournament in town. Being busy kept them both from feeling sad.

"We will still see each other?" Julia asked, accidentally making a question of what she intended to be a statement.

"I hope," Angela replied, accidentally making a statement of what she intended to be a question.

Marco's anger would activate without trick or trigger. A benign conversation about the geese migrating or dinner, for example, could catapult into a violent encounter. Angela missed her days at the motel.

Angry Marcos would grab a soft, fleshy part of her body—a thigh, bicep, forearm, pinch of breast—and give it all his stress, squeezing her body like he aimed to pop it. As he squeezed, Marcos verbalized Angela's fears as if that were his new art form, peppering her with spiny one-liners she could not unhear.

Marcos said she was not smart or strong enough to survive without him; he said the baby had already ruined her beauty, her body; he said he was the only person who would ever stoop to love her; he said Angela would be just like her mother one day.

Angela did not know how to react to Marcos's anger except to be very quiet until he was done with her. She closed her eyes and counted in her head to pass the time, imagining the numbers as bright pink neon signs flashing in the window of her mind.

Later, in the shower or while she changed clothes, she did not let her eyes linger on the mottled handprints, but with every splash of water or swish of fabric, she knew she was covered in him.

A bit of relief: Marcos disappeared for a few days, which was not unusual. Then a few days became two weeks, which was.

Marcos finally returned, his darkness subsided, and Angela reembraced the affirming and affable guy she fell for over the summer, the version of him she loved most.

Then the abrupt reversal—the good Marcos, once again, vanished, and the cranky Marcos resumed his stance. First the sulking, cynicism, and complaining. Then the insults, bickering, and abuse. But this time Angela decided she'd had enough. This time would be different. This time she would not take any of it.

"Stay," Marcos said, grabbing Angela's forearm when she tried to get up from bed.

Angela pulled away, and at the same time, Marcos loosened his grip. Angela hit the floor, landing with all her weight on the point of her elbow. They both heard the snap.

Angela wanted to wail but couldn't. She couldn't say anything.

"Your cheek is bleeding," Marcos said at last. "You must have scraped it on the door."

He helped her sit up, offered her a damp towel for her face, and then, pleased with his caring display, opted to go for a long swim.

A force beyond her own body and will propelled Angela's feet and carried her to the motel. She would barely remember walking through dusk into early night, stopping every few feet on the shoulder of the road, kneeling over when the pain made her head spin.

Angela collapsed on the couch in the lobby and called out for Patricia. Right away, Patricia noticed Angela's swollen arm resting limply on her belly.

"Can I stay here tonight? I'll pay you back. I'll work."

"Oh, no, you won't. I'll call Julia and fix you a room."

Patricia and Julia propped Angela up in bed with an ice pack from the machine down the hall and extra pillows from the supply room.

"How's that feel?" Julia asked.

"It feels like I have a beating heart in my arm," Angela said, groaning.

George came by with a handle of whiskey at some point in the evening. Angela didn't have any, but he and Julia did. Angela fell asleep listening to their voices, her head resting on Julia's shoulder.

"It's definitely fractured," the emergency room doctor said the next morning. But that would be obvious to anyone. Overnight, Angela's elbow and forearm had turned the deep shade of an eggplant.

"How did the injury occur?"

"I fell and landed wrong, wanted to protect the baby."

"I would say so. The mother's sacrifice." The doctor sighed. "All right, take deep breaths."

Julia held Angela's hand as the doctor put her in a cast that went up to her shoulder.

"You don't have to go back to him," Julia said after the doctor left the room. "We'll help with the baby, Angela. Come live with us. My family loves you."

For the first time since the ordeal began, Angela's face crumpled, but she would not let herself cry.

SCENE: Something Brief but Significant

George helps Angela get comfortable in Julia's bedroom.

GEORGE: Do you want me to set up the television in here?

ANGELA: You don't have to.

GEORGE: I want to.

ANGELA: I should try to rest.

GEORGE: Well, can I bring you a milkshake when I get off work?

ANGELA: That would be nice. Thank you.

GEORGE: Which flavor?

ANGELA: What flavor do you get?

GEORGE: I don't like milkshakes.

ANGELA: What does Julia like?

GEORGE: Strawberry, I think.

ANGELA: Strawberry's good. Thank you.

. . .

GEORGE: Would you like another blanket?

ANGELA: Sure.

GEORGE: I'll find one.

George disappears for a few minutes. Angela waits. He returns and covers her up with the new blanket. They touch somehow. It is brief but significant.

GEORGE: Are you in pain?

ANGELA: No.

GEORGE: Are you lying?

ANGELA: Yes.

They laugh, but laughing makes Angela hurt. So she bites the inside of her cheek and just smiles.

After the incident, Angela stayed in Julia's room, sleeping beside her in bed. One night, staring up at the dark ceiling after they turned off the lights, Angela thought aloud, "I wonder if he misses me."

"Do you *want* him to miss you?"

Angela could feel Julia's incredulous expression in the dark. "I don't know."

"Good god, Angela! He's pathetic. Let him go!"

Angela knew then that she had to keep some things to herself.

Certain sensations were no longer neutral. The smells of honeysuckle, campfire, and cigarette smoke, the sound of water lapping against rotten wood, the taste of wild blackberries, the texture of pilling flannel on her bare skin, and even the very thought of summer held powerful memories of Marcos. The Marcos who, for a time, loved, saved, and colored her life with hope and wonder. Angela couldn't tell which hurt more, her body or heart.

Despite her better sense, Angela missed Marcos so much.

When Angela could "pop any day now" (Julia's words), Julia and Theresa threw her a baby shower with the usual family group as well as Patricia and a few other girls from the motel.

At the party, George kept refilling Angela's punch glass when it was just a third empty, clearing away wrapping paper, and replenishing Angela's cookies and chips. People joked that George was her butler. Later, as he demonstrated a few much-improved magic tricks, Julia sensed something new.

Julia thought she knew George's mind better than he did. She thought they could share anything. Yet, right in front of everyone, Julia and George's connection was changing. Angela was making Julia's twin brother—who, until this moment, Julia had perceived as her truest equal—a man.

Angela gave birth at the end of February in the hospital, with Julia squeezing one hand and Theresa the other. When Angela thought she could not push anymore, Theresa told her to imagine herself as an Oklahoma wind, a fifty-mile-per-hour gust with enough power to rip the shingles off a roof, overturn a picnic table, or split a tree in two. A few minutes later, the three women met Angela's baby girl.

ngela named her daughter Wren after the small bird pecking at the ground beneath Julia's bedroom window while her elbow healed. The wren was missing its tail feathers, and while Angela healed, they grew back. Angela knew it was a common bird, but the fact that it showed up every day without fail made that singular specimen of the species extraordinary. Julia chose Wren's middle name, Ihullo, the Chickasaw word for *beloved*.

The first wonderful thing about Wren was that, except for her dark chocolate eyes, she looked just like her mother.

Loving Wren was easy, but everything else felt strange, new, and hard.

"You're doing great," Theresa told Angela and Wren, both half-dressed and in tears. "You are figuring things out together."

"I don't feel like we are."

"Here," Theresa said, opening her arms. "Let me have her for a few minutes while you take a shower."

Even with Theresa's affirmations, Angela worried she was doing the wrong things.

As they got used to each other, Angela's favorite time with Wren was late at night when the house was asleep. When Wren fussed, Angela rose from her mattress in the corner of the living room, lifted her from the hand-me-down crib, paced the room a few times, and nursed her on the sofa. Angela felt shy nursing in front of anyone but Theresa or Julia; living in crowded quarters made it challenging to find privacy when she needed it. At night, they could be themselves.

One of those nights, Wren did a small, marvelous thing: she found Angela's ordinary index finger and chose to reach for her over the world's trillion interesting objects.

Then the interminable ache, the sadness, bundled up with every single day now that she was a mother. Often a single morning felt like six months, but a week zipped by in a blink.

Time was a heavy stone turning inside her. Wren, everything, changed so fast.

A BRIEF INTERLUDE

At some point in every semester, Lewis would get frustrated during rehearsal and stomp across the stage yelling something like:

> *Don't just stand there! React!*
> *Objective!*
> *Objective!*
> *Objective!*
> *Unless your character is enlightened,*
> *you want something in every scene!*
> *At least* try *to get it.*

Of course, Lewis was not truly frustrated with his students. He was dissatisfied with himself and saw his students' failure as his own pedagogical shortcoming.

"Why is the difference between practice and theory so hard to explain?" Lewis thought aloud as Wren poured him a glass of wine after rehearsal one night.

"Well, maybe in real life, people don't have an objective. Not an obvious one, anyway. And that's why the concept is hard to put into practice."

"Everyone has an objective."

"Not everyone."

"Who are you thinking of, then?"

"My mother, I suppose."

"That wasn't her fault."

"You never knew her. She could have accomplished *something* in the time she had left."

"Wren. She did something amazing."

"And what was that?"

"She raised you."

When Angela returned to her job at the Cross Timbers, Marcos waited for her in the parking lot after her shifts, wooing her with compliments and flooding her with increasingly eccentric expressions of remorse. At first Angela remained strong, ignoring Marcos even as he chased after George's truck like a dog. But eventually, Marcos's perseverance weakened her resolve. Angela wanted to try again.

Julia and Theresa looked at Angela fixedly, lips pursed, brows furrowed in an identical way, as Angela elucidated a few insubstantial reasons why it was a good idea to move back with him.

"And Wren deserves to grow up in a family," Angela concluded.

"But we are your family," Julia replied.

Angela's body did not trust Marcos, even though her mind wanted very much to begin again. Every time Marcos touched her, Angela had to resist the impulse to get far away from him.

Meanwhile, Marcos became afflicted with a fussy, mercurial boredom. His moods were more unpredictable than the baby's.

Marcos heard about an uprising of communal living groups in New Mexico and began making plans to move to one of these places, sight unseen.

"I've become too comfortable. I've outgrown this life. Or maybe it's just fate, the universe calling me elsewhere, this falling out of love," Marcos said.

"What if you don't like it there?" Angela asked.

Marcos rolled his eyes; he believed he had an infinite number of lives to try on and discard.

When Julia and her family heard the news about Marcos leaving, they were a word beyond relieved. They were *elated*.

Because Julia watched so many lawyers on TV, she encouraged Angela to ask for the boat title instead of child support.

"You won't get a dime out of him, ever," Julia said.

"You think?" Angela replied.

"Uh, yeah. Better negotiate what you can up front before he becomes untraceable."

Marcos agreed to Angela's terms. He even seemed relieved by them, like Angela had given him a very good deal. Marcos then became single-minded in his preparations for a free and unencumbered life.

The morning Marcos left for New Mexico, his truck packed with art supplies, tools, fishing poles, and books about recondite spiritualities, he held his daughter for the last time, as if she were a strange, wild animal. Marcos promptly returned the baby to her mother. Angela turned her face when he leaned in for a kiss.

"Don't touch me, Marcos. We're not like that anymore."

Wren started to fuss, and Angela bounced her on a hip until she settled. Marcos looked on as if he were a little boy, a helpless victim to adult choices.

"Don't you think everything happens for a reason?" Marcos asked, hoping Angela would, once again, sit at his feet; lap up his recited, unlived wisdom; carry his broken world on her young shoulders.

Wind, wind, wind, wind, wind, wind, Angela thought.

"No. I don't." The back of her neck tingled, and Angela got a sudden, strong inner directive to run.

Angela wrapped her arms around Wren and moved as fast as she could across the parking lot, through the marina, and to the boat.

Once inside, Angela locked the doors, put Wren down in her crib, and collapsed on the floor, adrenaline pulsing.

Meanwhile, Marcos sat in his truck for twenty minutes, paralyzed by fear. *What am I doing?* he thought. He craved comfort and simultaneously found himself filled with turbulent fury.

Just as Marcos put his hand on the door handle to march back to the houseboat *(to give Angela a piece of my mind!),* a foreign consciousness entered his mind.

273

Leave her be, it said, *just drive away.*

Marcos retracted, put the key in the ignition, and barreled down the road toward the highway, onward to New Mexico, leaving behind a cloud of gravel dust that only time and gravity could settle.

Angela had been grieving Marcos almost as long as she'd known him, and finally, like a rainbow against a bruise-hued cloud, she saw the real Marcos—not as an idea, dream, hope, or possibility—but as he really was.

Marcos drew an outline of a person who was generous, wise, and kind, and Angela's longing animated his image with life and color. This two-dimensional Marcos, the one she imagined, was never real.

Yet the heartbreak was not for nothing. Angela would be left with a gift, a life, her daughter.

*F*all and winter pass. Wren turns one. Angela, Julia, and George are all a few months shy of seventeen and nineteen, respectively. The three teenagers and baby become a new foursome who do everything together. Now, once again, early spring:

They would strap Wren in a carrier on George's back because he was the tallest, farther away from ticks, stubbly mesquite trees, and greenbrier, and the three of them would trek through the tall grass down to the river. With his long strides, George couldn't help walking far ahead of the girls, having deep (albeit one-sided) conversations with Wren, while Julia and Angela brought up the rear.

"Each ring is a year in the life of this tree. And the width of the ring tells us how much water the tree got that year," George said, guiding Wren's hand over a washed-up tree stump.

"George, she can't understand you," Angela said, amused. (George talked to Wren like an adult instead of using a baby voice, like everyone else.)

"How do you know?"

"Well, she's only one year old."

"In human years," said George, now flying Wren above his head like a hawk.

"Yes, George. Human years. That's how we measure!" Julia exclaimed, taking Wren from his arms.

Later, when Julia went for a walk down the beach with Wren in the carrier, George tried the same counting exercise with Angela. Hand over hand, finger on finger, they counted the rings. In the end, the true age was quite disputed, as Angela felt ring numbers 108 and 109 were one ring, number 108, while George felt they were defined enough to call them separate rings.

It wasn't a true disagreement about the age of the tree but, rather, a vehicle to hold hands and explore the wondrous conundrum of having more words to say to the other than there were seconds in the day.

Theresa babysat Wren while Angela was at work, and in exchange, Angela helped Theresa with chores.

As Angela and George's friendship flirted with the border of romance, they tried to keep their exploration private, which proved to be quite challenging, because they were so often surrounded by people at the house.

Angela wanted to tell Julia everything: how her brother was a wonderful, kind person, how she felt safe, how George made her laugh. But a harshness in Julia's energy whenever her brother's name came up made Angela hold back.

Of course, Julia knew.

JULIA'S EVIDENCE

The first intimation: George and Angela, gawking at each other in the Cross Timbers parking lot the first time they met. George, unusually quiet, spoke and smiled with his lips covering his teeth (meaning he wanted to look good). Angela stood on her tippy-toes to talk to him (meaning she wanted to be understood).

Christmas Eve: George and his disastrous magic tricks; Angela, trying not to laugh at him like everyone else. Later, they ran off in the dark together for an hour (doing who knows what). George drove Angela home (alone).

The baby shower: George, eager and helpful; Angela, dazed and delighted; her punch glass, always full.

The tree stump day: some awfully flirtatious handholding and giggling, clearly basking in the euphoric fumes of infatuation. At supper the same evening, Julia saw them holding hands beneath the table.

Fact #1: Angela looked for George whenever she entered a room.

Fact #2: George opened a savings account.

Fact #3: Angela cut bangs and started wearing blue eyeshadow.

Fact #4: George grew a mustache.

Fact #5: Angela blushed whenever she said his name.

The change seemed invisible at first. So they separately convinced themselves it was not happening. But the wedge of silence between them grew, and their uncomplicated friendship began to crack.

Julia longed for Angela, and then she hated her.

Meanwhile, George's orbit recalibrated. When he wasn't working at the tractor dealership, his growing avidity for Angela and Wren lured him to the marina.

He surprised Angela with strawberry milkshakes and Cokes from the Bait 'N Tackle Shop. He played with Wren while Angela did chores or took a nap. He created projects to give himself reasons to stick around—caulking, painting, cabinetry, cleaning.

Angela admitted she was worried about Wren falling in the water without a life vest before she could swim, so George started reinforcing the railing and adding extra locks to the door and gate.

"I didn't used to think about things like this," Angela said with a sigh.

Their eyes mutually found Wren, who was occupied with her favorite toy, a stuffed bear with a missing eye.

"Me, neither," George replied, grinning.

"Why are you smiling?"

A pair of ducks zipped toward a cluster of cattails; in the distance, a fishman reeled in a catfish; a red-tailed hawk surveyed the ground for vermin above their heads; the breeze moved a tuft of hair out of Angela's eyes; Wren babbled something incoherent but cheerful to the air or her bear. This was the life surrounding him, the life he loved, the life he was choosing. George wanted to unmask, to leap into the sky, to free-fall, to say the real thing:

"I like you," George began.

"I like you, too. You're a great friend," Angela replied.

"Well, friends is one thing, but I wanted
to ask—
would you like
to be more than friends?
Like,
I'm thinking,
my girlfriend?

And before you say anything, I want you to know
I've been making plans.
I want to get us a motor for the boat so we can take it out on the water.
I found a guy who'll give me a good deal
once I have the money to pay 'em.
And I'm starting classes at the community college this fall.
I'm gonna be a businessman one day, Angela.
And we're gonna live in a house
with two stories
and a garage
and maybe even a coupla trees.
My whole life, I've wanted something good,
and I think you and Wren are it.
Just wanted to tell you that."

Angela and Wren, each from her respective vantage, happened to look at him with the same open-eyed expression.

"What do you think?" George asked, both afraid and aching to know her answer.

"I've always wanted to take the boat out," Angela replied.

"Good," George said, relieved, leaning in. "Me, too."

They kissed, just once.

George did not ask to spend the night. They were still teenagers, just a couple of kids who had only ever kissed and held hands, with plenty of time to grow up together, plenty of time for all the rest.

That night, Angela recalled the first time she got high with Marcos, which now seemed so long ago. Marcos was right about one thing. She was alone in the world, but now her aloneness was linked to Wren, who, even as a toddler, seemed to know she was her own whole person.

While Wren slept on a pillow of silken hair, Angela murmured an invocation for herself, for her daughter, for all that had passed, and for all that was to come:

"Someday, when you're far from here,
maybe you'll think of this place.

Maybe you'll miss our friend of a lake rocking you to sleep, to peace.
I used to dream of a guy,
a guy that would take me away from all my problems,
make me whole, make me right.
Now I think the dream is being held through the night
by something beautiful on this Earth.
And we are, you and me, together
in our little boat on this big lake
nestled in the cradle of the world."

George, perfectly content watching the moon rise and reflect on the water instead of the television; George, persisting with magic tricks, trying to improve; George, walking slow so Angela can keep up with his long strides; George, fearless and eagerly holding almost any kind of snake, toad, lizard, or salamander with his bare hands; George, clapping and cheering as Wren takes her first steps—*Go, my girl, go,* he says. Angela beams at both of them.

A tense thickness in the air, a jaundiced sky, and an eerie sudden silence—
no birds, no breeze—mean one thing in an Oklahoma May.

And sure enough, at a quarter to four o'clock, the tornado sirens blared.
For locals, this was no shock, just a regular Tuesday in the spring, and
chances were good they would all be home for dinner.

All the Cross Timbers staff and guests crowded into the hallway on the
first floor where they would be most protected if a twister touched down.
Angela and Julia slipped out the side door to watch the storm develop from
beneath the awning. (Like the child who passes an index finger through
a candle flame to test the boundary between peace and pain, people who
grow up in Tornado Alley know when to linger and when to run for their
lives.)

"No one at the house answered the phone. I've called twice," Angela
said.

"I promise they're all in the shelter," Julia replied. "Wren's fine."

"Are you sure?"

"Yes."

"I hope you're right."

"I know I am."

A wall cloud unleashed a few soft tendrils, reaching for the earth. The
afternoon sky turned dark as coal. The wind started to pick up, thrashing
treetops and whipping their hair into fine spears. A period of torrential
rain followed by globules of penny-sized hail. Then a hush. Moving toward
them: the regal dark column, hungry for the good life, ready to receive the
objects of the world.

"We should go in," Julia said. Angela nodded in agreement, but they
stayed, watching the hail until Patricia rapped on the door, poked her head
out, and ordered them to take shelter inside.

*   *   *

Across Jefferson, Carter, and Love counties, human bodies cowered into one another. For thirty swollen minutes, they waited for something to happen.

Angela thought in prayer, wishing she were with Wren and George and Theresa and even her parents, wherever, however, they were. Without a task to occupy their hands or a baby to distract them, Angela and Julia had little to say to each other.

Longing for closeness, for that old feeling of connection, Angela blurted, "I've been seeing George." She regretted it immediately, realizing she had revealed this information in the wrong way: without George, in a public place, during a harrowing hour.

"I know, *Angela,*" Julia snarled. Angela's name was a wad of gristle in her mouth. "I've known for a long time."

"Really?"

"Don't be *stupid*. You've been obvious all along."

The radio announced the tornado would travel north, away from them. For those lucky few, the storm was over.

The hallway sighed.

A few minutes later, Angela and Julia returned to work and did not speak for the rest of their shift.

A few hours later, Angela, George, and Julia shared an extremely quiet drive home.

So, the atmospheric shimmering of greatest happiness, two girls greeting life hand in hand, was theirs to borrow, not keep.

Angela and Julia's ending was one of decay, not shattering, a vague and gradual slipping away. Angela would puzzle over the mystery even many years later, never quite understanding what happened, or when, exactly, their friendship ended.

Even though their breakup lacked gravitas, Julia left an aching hollow. For the rest of her life, whenever Angela thought of Julia, she would ruminate on the same tired questions:

When had the instigating fissure occurred?

Why had neither of them done anything to repair it?

Were they meant only to share a moment and pass on, alone, taking opposite forks on the road to womanhood?

"Cooo," Wren said, pointing to the cousins' puppy, chewing on someone's work boot in the yard.

Angela and George almost levitated.

"Is that a *dog*?" Angela asked.

Wren pointed again at the dog. "Cooo."

"Did you say dog? Do you want to pet it?"

George flashed Angela a look that said, *Don't let her.* (Its full, black-tipped tail and long jawline made everyone think it was part coyote.)

"Cooo," Wren repeated.

"I wonder what she'll say next," George wondered. "I suppose it could be anything," George replied to himself, his habit.

"You always forget that she's just a baby," Angela said.

"I wouldn't underestimate her," George replied. "If she's anything like her mom. Right, Wren?"

"Coooo," Wren chimed, possibly agreeing.

Angela woke at quarter to six the next morning to Wren babbling something that resembled the word *mama*.

"Yes, that's me," Angela replied, smiling, as she lifted Wren from her crib.

As she changed Wren's diaper minutes later, Angela's right elbow retracted and tightened, the joint feeling more like a spring than a hinge. For a few hours, Angela could not fully straighten her arm, but her elbow relaxed as the day progressed, and the incident slipped from her mind.

Throughout the fall, Angela woke up exhausted every morning, even though Wren was sleeping through the night.

Angela decided it must have something to do with the nightmares she was having about her mother, which followed her into the next day like tree sap.

Colleen, drunk as ever, flying down the highway in a red convertible until she drove herself right off a cliff, while Angela, unable to get her attention in the backseat, screamed "STOP, STOP, STOP—"

The separation anxiety began a few months after Wren turned two. Every time Angela left Wren with Theresa, Wren would throw herself at the window facing the road, press her face to the glass, and wail as she watched George's truck drive off with Angela in it.

One of these times, Angela could not resist the anguished, bellowing face and asked George to stop the car while she ran back to the house to give Wren another hug.

As Angela held her tearful girl and told her what she always did ("You're going to read books and play with our good friend Theresa, and it will be so fun"), her arm involuntarily contracted around Wren's neck. Wren could not even get enough oxygen to scream. Her cheeks turned red and then, alarmingly, blue.

"George! Theresa! Help!" Angela yelled, and they came running from different directions. "My arm is locked. I can't get it off her neck. She can't breathe!"

George wrestled with Angela's arm while Theresa held on to Wren's torso, and when it was all over, the four of them sat in a heap on the grass, gasping, afraid, and confused.

"Aren't you Dr. Wyatt's daughter?" a nurse with big blond bangs asked as she read Angela's blood pressure.

Angela felt a sting just hearing his name. "Yes, that's my father."

"How is he doing?"

Angela thought of the last time she saw her parents, three months ago, after the mediation, when her parents divided her childhood between themselves. They met Wren with tentative arms on the steps of her childhood home, and afterward, Angela's father gave her money.

At the time, Angela wanted nothing to do with either of her parents, and her parents, wanting nothing to do with each other, put their attention on Angela. This ripple of rejection upset everyone but Wren, who found a turtle in the grass and wouldn't let it be.

"He's fine," Angela replied.

"And your mom? Haven't seen Colleen in ages," the nurse pried.

"She's doing all right, too."

Colleen already had a fiancé in Arizona. She sent Angela postcards with pictures of the Southwest, writing brief messages in her loopy handwriting:

Come visit, doll!
xoxoxoxo, MOM

"That's good to hear. I thought I heard from somewhere y'all were having a hard time." The nurse revealed her intention to cross the thin line from small talk to prying. "And who's this little cutie you're babysitting?"

Wren, sticky with applesauce, was playing with a toy car on the floor.

"This is my daughter, Wren."

"Daughter?"

Angela could see the nurse's thinking plastered on her face, putting together the facts of Angela's broken family so she could share her speculations with whomever she encountered next. *You wouldn't believe what I learned today. Do you remember Dr. Wyatt? . . .*

And this was why Angela had grown to prefer being in the country, an expansive horizon with more cows than people, to a suffocating small town fueled by people's sad stories.

"What's going on today, Ms. Angela?" the doctor asked a few minutes later.

"I'm having some trouble with my arm. Sometimes it cramps, and I can't straighten it for hours. I fractured my elbow about two years ago. I'm sure it's something to do with that. Don't you think?"

After the doctor examined her joints, he performed a complete physical and asked questions that, to Angela's mind, had nothing to do with her issue.

How is your temperature regulation? Do you find it difficult to get warm when it is cold or stay cool when it's hot out? Have you noticed any changes in your sense of smell? What about your vision? Hearing? How long have your eyes been bloodshot? Would you say that you have persistently dry skin? Did you know your tongue has a small fork in it?

"I'm going to refer you to Dr. Park, a specialist in Oklahoma City. You are showing classic markers of a reptilian mutation."

Wren waved to get Angela's attention. "Go now?"

"What are you talking about? A mutation? What markers?" Angela asked, feeling suddenly confused and frantic.

"Dr. Park will be much better equipped to go over your test results, provide answers to specific questions, and create a treatment plan."

Angela went to her appointment with Dr. Park while George took Wren to Sonic for a slush.

After a physical examination, Dr. Park slapped Angela's file down on the counter.

"Fortunately, we've caught your Varanus komodoensis mutation very early," said Dr. Park, who loved her job. "Do you have any questions?"

"Is there a cure?"

"There's no cure, but you have a lot of treatment options to manage the symptoms."

"Is it contagious?"

"Mutations are not contagious, but we do know the disease runs in families. It typically skips a generation. Grandparent to grandchild, so on and so forth."

"How long until . . . ?"

"Until the mutation completes?"

Angela nodded. Dr. Park squinted at Angela. To Dr. Park, Angela was not a person but, rather, a puzzle.

"At your stage, about twenty years. Reptilian mutations have a very slow progression rate. Do you have any other questions?"

Angela shook her head.

"Today I'd like to discuss your treatment plan. We'll start you off on two different medications to regulate body temperature, relax the joints, and mitigate any skin irritation you may be experiencing . . ."

As Dr. Park explained the side effects of the various medications, Angela got distracted by the lizard anatomy poster on the wall. Then she thought of Wren and George and felt her optimistic future disintegrating, revealing a truer calamitous one. It all seemed unreal.

"Well, that's it from me today. It has been a pleasure to meet you, Ms. Wyatt," Dr. Park concluded. "After you change out of the gown, our keeper will give you a tour of the facility. Tell Cathy at the front desk that I want to see you again in two months, but please do not hesitate to reach out if something comes up sooner."

Then the click of a very specific door, a click Angela would hear again and again through the years. A click that meant she was one appointment closer to the end of it all.

The keeper, a man with the physique of a bodybuilder, met Angela outside the facility, a cinder-block building the size of a gymnasium. He handed her a glossy pamphlet entitled "What to Expect," with a stoic physician holding a Komodo dragon by a chain-link leash pictured on the front.

When the keeper and Angela passed, five Komodo dragons, locked up like shelter dogs, growled, hissed, grunted, and scaled their cages with their sharp claws. Some opened their mouths wide, revealing long, forked tongues. They all had at least one human feature. Hand, nose, neck, calf, foot.

As the keeper explained the protocols for feeding and visitation, he noticed Angela reading the name tag above the lock on each cage: Penelope, Tommy, Ellen, Lorenzo, and Barb.

"Today is Penelope's birthday. We'll have a little party when her family gets here later this afternoon. And Barb will be going to her placement tomorrow."

"What is placement?" Angela asked.

The keeper rolled up his sleeves, revealing a prolific number of scars on his arms.

"Placement is where we release these animals when they complete their mutations. For these guys, it's Indonesia. Which reminds me, we offer complimentary placement transport if you begin a payment plan within six months of diagnosis. All the prices are listed in your pamphlet."

Angela wished—as was now a habit when life overwhelmed her—that she could beam herself into the stars.

"What if I don't want to go to a placement?"

The keeper nodded sympathetically, which gave Angela the feeling that he expected this question.

"Then the U.S. Department of Health and Human Services requires a regulated facility, like this one, to perform a humane execution. You are now in our records, and we are required to report all new data."

Much later, after George left and Wren was asleep, Angela retrieved the pamphlet from the bottom of her purse. She had lied to George after the appointment, telling him her test results were inconclusive. Really, Angela just needed some time alone to make sense of things.

As Angela flipped through the glossy pages, she realized there were so many questions she could have asked, questions the pamphlet did not address.

How do I protect others when I become venomous? What does it feel like to crawl with four legs instead of walk with two? What will people think when I look like a prehistoric animal with a tail longer than my body and a head that is flat and small? What will it be like to own nothing, know no one, and live completely outdoors? When will I stop becoming new versions of myself but something else? Will I be able to care for Wren? And the worst: Will Wren have to care for me?

WHAT TO EXPECT:
VARANUS KOMODOENSIS MUTATION

STAGE 1:
- Joint stiffness and contractions
- Temperature irregularities (inability to stay warm or cool)
- Tongue tenderness
- Loose teeth

STAGE 2:
- Appetite changes (desire for larger but less frequent meat-based meals)
- Scales begin to replace human skin
- Short-term memory loss
- Teeth falling out

STAGE 3:
- The ability to smell minuscule amounts of blood across distances
- Farsightedness
- Beginning of tongue lengthening and splitting
- Cessation of menses (females)

STAGE 4:
- Periodically lays eggs (females)
- Rapid body mutation (legs, torso, tail, and head)
- Growth of new teeth
- Development of venomous glands
- Continuation of tongue lengthening and splitting

STAGE 5:
- Ability to climb trees
- Ability to run at least 10 mph

- Profound memory loss
- Loss of ability to speak and understand language
- Loss of motor abilities
- Loss of impulse control

Call your provider's emergency line if:
- Your body temperature rises above 105° or falls below 90°
- You feel you may become a danger to yourself or others

SCENE: I Love Them All

GEORGE: Please don't break up with me. I don't understand. Why?

ANGELA: You deserve so much more
   than me.

GEORGE: I don't give a flyin' fig about your mutation, Angela!
   It doesn't change how I feel about you.
   You are not your mother.
   You are your own person,
   and I love you.
   . . .
   I love you, Angela.
   I want to build a life together.
   I want to be her father.
   Hell, let's get married today.
   What do you say?

Angela mentally extracts herself from the scene by imagining bits of herself aloft and floating, dandelion seeds in outer space. Here, pain and conse-quences are in the world beyond her, and the world beyond her is a marble within which she is but a fleck inside a fleck inside a fleck inside a fleck inside a fleck.

GEORGE: Please, Angela.
 Just look at me.
 Don't you see who I am?
 I love reptiles.
 I love them all.

George would always feel Angela had been the great love of his life. His love never transformed into anger or faded to neutrality. From afar, George wanted the very best for Angela. He never stopped caring or thinking about her.

When George saw Wren twenty years later at Angela's memorial service, he introduced himself as an old friend of her mother's.

"Your mom was a strong and wonderful woman," George said, overwhelmed by Wren's staggering resemblance to Angela.

"How did you know her?"

"We were friends as teenagers but drifted apart."

"That happens."

George reached into his jacket pocket and handed Wren a square of paper torn from the memorial service program with his name and phone number scrawled on it.

"I know you don't know me, but please give me a call if I can ever help you. Day or night. I really mean it."

"Thank you. That's very kind."

"Your mother would be so proud of you," he said, choking up, but the truth was, George was getting emotional because he was proud, too.

Wren, age six

"Mom, where do people go when they die?"
"Nobody knows."
"Well, what does it *feel like* to die?" Wren pushed.
"I don't know."
"Yes, you do."
"I'm not dying.
I'm *changing*.
Dying is similar to changing,
but dying and changing are also very different."
"Different how?"
"I don't know." Angela sighed.
"What do I do if I miss you?"
"When I die?"
"No, when you *change*. You just said *not dying*."
. . .
"Well,
when you miss me,
you'll go somewhere big and open,
a place like our lake
or any place where you can see the whole sky.
Once you're there, take a big, deep breath,
and start to notice all the things we notice when we're together."
"Like birds?"

"Yes, notice the cardinals, the scissor-tailed flycatchers . . ."
"And the hummingbirds, robins, and red-bellied woodpeckers?"
"Yes, and the clouds, moon, and stars.
And the sounds of things,
like the breeze in the tall grass,
the wind in the trees,
the whir of cars passing on the interstate,
people talking, yelling, laughing.
Smell the campfire smoke,
summer rain,
wet leaves.
But most of all, I want you to notice what's inside you.
Ask yourself, *What do I need?*"
"Okay."
"Try it now. Close your eyes. Ask yourself—"
"—what do I need?" Wren squeezed her eyes closed. "Prolly ice cream."
"You're darn right. Always."
"Always."

Wren, age seven

Angela was not sure how much Wren understood or what was appropriate to share with her. Already, Wren had noticed things Angela wished she hadn't, things that frightened her small girl.

Angela wore pants and long sleeves to cover the scales forming on her limbs, but Wren knew what was beneath the fabric.

"Does it itch?" Wren asked.

"Sometimes."

"Does it hurt?"

"Sometimes."

Wren kissed the gray-green patch on Angela's wrist, creeping out from her shirt sleeve. "Feel better now?"

"Yes, very much."

Then Wren wanted to see the other scaly patches on her mother's body so she could update her secret mental inventory.

Angela rolled up her sleeves and pant legs to show her.

Wren seemed fine, like her usual self, the rest of the afternoon, but right before bed, just as Angela turned off the light, Wren asked in the most pained, grasping way: *"Mommy, are you still real?"*

Wren, age eight

With help from her dad, Angela bought a car to replace their increasingly unreliable truck.

"What do you think?" Angela asked Wren, who was standing with her hands on her hips, like a discerning adult.

"It's my favorite color."

"I thought your favorite color was red."

"I just changed it to blue. To match."

Angela and Wren took the new car out for a drive. They drove so far out that the roads were marked with numbered stakes in the ground rather than perpendicular green street signs. On either side of the dirt road, a broad big-skyed flatness, grass and sky kissing at the end of the world.

"I want to talk to you about The Change," Angela said, turning down the radio. The Change was code for Angela's mutation.

"Not now," Wren replied to the passenger window instead of her mother.

"We don't have to have a conversation, but I do need you to listen."

"Fine."

"I am having trouble with my short-term memory, which means I may not remember things like appointments, directions, or stories from your day. I could even forget people's names. I need you to listen very closely, because you might have to help me remember things sometimes."

"Will you remember who I am?" Wren asked in a clenched voice, a voice that always made Angela feel like she'd just tripped on an uneven sidewalk.

Angela pulled over in front of a cattle guard.

"If it ever seems like I have forgotten,
remember my voice right here,
and know that I do remember.
I will always know who you are."

Wren, age ten

It is the year Wren watches *The Wizard of Oz* almost every day after school.

It is the year Angela sells the houseboat, and with money from the sale plus more from her father, the family of two moves to a three-room house in the country with enough sky to keep one entertained for a lifetime or more.

It is the year Angela and Wren become two kids loose on the world.

It is the year they climb over Do Not Trespass signs and run through fields of sunflowers triple Wren's height, look up to their drooping, dappled heads, and see not only the seeding part of the plant but also the many faces of a benevolent, adjusting God.

It is the year Angela enters Stage 3 of her mutation.

It is the year Angela starts craving wild game and goes bowhunting in the backyard for anything in season.

It is the year Wren skips two grades in math; she is still the best in the class.

It is the year Angela's tongue begins to drastically lengthen and fork down the center.

It is the year Angela develops sudden overwhelming urges to crawl. The impulse strikes anywhere—in the grocery store, at a parent-teacher conference, at work, while cooking dinner—and she has to contain the energy building within her until she can unleash it privately, writhing and thrashing on the floor.

It is the year Wren begins to mother her mother.

It is the year Wren and Angela lose their molars in the same week. Wren's, to be replaced by her adult teeth. Angela's, to be replaced with sharp, retractable Komodo dragon ones. The tooth fairy comes for each of them, leaving behind deer antlers, special rocks, motel pens, and always, a note beneath their pillows:

> *Thank you for the tooth! Don't forget to brush the new one.*
> *Yours,*
> *The Tooth Fairy*

Wren, age eleven

In 1992, Wren and Angela stood at the doorways of separate but significant physiological changes. Wren, of puberty. Angela, of reptilian mutation. They were mutually awkward around both topics.

Wren did not go careening into womanhood as Angela had at the same age. Wren was a slow bloomer. For Angela, this was a relief. Her daughter's body was not dangerous, as her own was.

Angela blamed her body as the primary cause for her hardships, first the unplanned pregnancy as a teenager, and through the rest of her adulthood, the mutation. How was it that her self's container, her only true protection from the world's elements, had only ever betrayed her, surprised her, and enforced uncertainty and strangeness?

It was cliché but necessary that Angela found enduring solace in the stars. She did not contemplate the presence of mystery or infinity. Instead, Angela appreciated the cosmos's relative constancy.

Angela and Wren interpreted the night sky in their own way, drawing and naming constellations. It was their secret language, an orbiting, silent elegy. For example, the Big and Little Dippers were two kites flying next to each other. Angela and Wren pretended they held the kite strings, keeping the taut universe floating.

Wren, age sixteen

Breathless, Wren hid in her bedroom closet behind the reinforced metal door they'd installed one solemn Super Bowl Sunday two years ago. Beyond the closet, she locked her bedroom door and barricaded it with her desk and chair. Wren had enough water and nonperishable food inside the closet to last a few days. They had planned for this situation if—when—Angela became violent and unable to control her impulses.

In case you need protection, Angela had said at the time. Neither of them could imagine the scenario.

But now it was real. Danger, her mother—venomous, hungry, pacing the hallway.

During the last visitation, Wren had avoided telling Genevieve, their social worker, how quickly her mother had declined in recent months. Wren did not want to live in a foster home; she took care of herself. Wren also did not want her mother to live in a facility; she took care of her, too.

They still had good days together, great ones, even. Evenings when they climbed onto the roof to watch a brilliant sunset or celestial event; mornings when Angela made pancakes with fresh-picked blackberries, remembering how much Wren loved them; afternoons when they lazed about, reading, watching television, talking about anything and everything until they both got sleepy enough for a nap.

Yet this was not a good day.

When Angela broke down Wren's bedroom door, the entire house rattled. Angela tried to topple the reinforced closet door, too, but couldn't thanks to their planning and precautions. This seemed to make Angela even more determined, frustrated, and angry. Angela's claws screeched as they struck the metal door, making Wren shiver. Angela flitted her tongue through the crack at the bottom door, and Wren pressed herself against the farthest wall against a rack of shirts, so the tongue could not reach her.

Eventually, her mother lost interest and went into another room. Wren stayed in the closet, terrified, until she decided to risk an escape, plotting her steps before she left safety. Wren bolted through the house, grabbed the car keys and her bag, sprinted to the car parked alongside the house, jammed the key in the ignition, and drove—

Wren went farther than she needed to find safety, driving sixty in a thirty-five zone until she was at the high school. The football stadium was lit up for one of the final games of the season. *Touchdown,* the announcer boomed. The home team crowd cheered, punctuated by the marching band.

Parked in front of the auditorium, Wren dialed Dr. Park's twenty-four-hour line on her flip phone.

"I need to speak with Dr. Park as soon as possible." Wren's voice quivered.

"Yes, it's regarding my mother, Angela Wyatt—

. . .

This is her daughter, Wren.

. . .

Yes, Wren Wyatt. I'm authorized to call on her behalf.

. . .

Tell Dr. Park it's an emergency.
She needs a higher dose of her medication.
I'm not sure which one.

. . .

Yes, that's the right number.

. . .

Just tell Dr. Park to call back soon.
My mother has not been well."

Wren, age nineteen

After an encouraging stretch of relative stability, Angela ate a golden retriever. Wren happened to be home, visiting from college.

"I think it was a stray," Angela croaked. Her face was a mask of blood and fur, and her tongue hung past her chin, dripping bloody saliva onto the khaki dress she used to wear to work.

"*Mom*. It was a family pet." Wren held up a bloodied collar clinking with heart-shaped metal tags.

"Please forgive me."

"Don't apologize to me. Next time you feel the need to slaughter someone's pet, *tell me*, and I'll happily defrost some venison."

Wren did not see her mother as a sick woman living within a body she no longer knew or controlled. Instead, she saw a pathetic, powerless beast surrounded by murder, a mess of blood and guts. As rage bubbled up and spilled over, Wren sharpened a pernicious, worded arrow and lobbed it at the bull's-eye, her mother.

"*You are a monster.*"

Her mother's face and head fell in succession.

"I know," Angela whispered. "I know. I am."

Satisfied, Wren knew her arrow had hit the mark. And she knew it had hurt. But Wren did not know that she had also deflated the ever shrinking remnant of her mother who was fighting to hang on, fighting to remain in the world just to be near her daughter.

Wren did not speak to her mother for two days. And then the visit was over. Wren returned to her college life and tried to put the terrible incident behind her.

Wren, age twenty-four

The precise day Angela became a wild animal is hard to say. It might have been the day she ate a nest of cockroaches behind a McDonald's dumpster and then two pounds of stolen hamburger meat. Or the time she dug a hole through the sofa upholstery with her teeth and claws. Or when she stopped bathing. Or when she stopped speaking. Or when she stopped listening. Or when she stopped loving, at least in the way Wren knew her mother to love. Or when Angela forgot everything and everyone, even Wren.

The last time Wren saw her mother, she was devouring state-provided roadkill at the facility, absent from the world around her. Somehow the woman who did not like her peas, mashed potatoes, and fried catfish to touch on the plate was also the reptile slurping intestines off a concrete floor. Her mother ate every scrap, even fur and bones.

Wren did not want this to be her final memory, but here it was. This was it: mother and daughter, together, at the end.

Angela climbed the front wall of her cage, hissing and rattling the steel. On her hind legs, front claws hooked onto the bars to hold her upright, Angela towered over Wren, ten feet tall. Her twirling forked tongue snaked out of the cage, reaching for her daughter, fresh meat just out of reach.

"Mom, if you can understand me,

if you're listening,

if you're here:

I love you, I love you, I love you.

Thank you for everything, my whole life.
And please forgive me.
You did not deserve what I said.
You are not a monster.
You are not a beast.
You are the kindest, gentlest, strongest—
You are the most wonderful being
I have ever, ever known."

Wren signaled to the keeper that she was ready to leave for the final time. She took a last look at the woman who raised her. The woman who taught her how to read when she was four, how to flip over a tipped canoe, how to patch and embroider a hole in a pair of jeans so they looked more special than a brand-new pair, how to ignore the voices of those who claimed to have better ideas than her own. This was the woman who taught her to go beyond their small town even though she had never done so herself. Her mother, who laughed so loud it echoed in the halls of the Cross Timbers Motel. Her mother, who could drive anything but chose to walk, even in terrible weather, so she could observe the world changing slowly with the seasons. Her mother, who made the most delicious pancakes and baked bread from scratch. Her mother, who could identify every bird by name and call. Her mother, who could grow a garden in an eggshell. Her mother, the kindest person she would ever know. Her mother, her mother, her mother, her mother, her mother. Her mother, an animal, whose eyes were filled with blood.

PART THREE

LEWIS WOODARD and MARGARET C. FINNEGAN

MAIN CHARACTERS

LEWIS: Carcharodon carcharias; often stubborn, irritable, heartbroken, and homesick, Lewis was formerly a man with an excellent sense of humor.

MARGARET C. FINNEGAN: Carcharodon carcharias; chock-full of ocean expertise yet inexperienced in matters of the heart. Raised by a dolphin pod and Billy and Carolyn Finnegan of Dayton, Ohio. Prefers to be called by her full name because it reminds Margaret of her mother, Carolyn, who liked sounding the full percussive nature of Margaret's name, the reverberations floating like a soft cloud above a spring green meadow in the place Margaret once lived a very long time ago.

SETTING

Various oceans. Present.

NOTE

Please find in the following pages a story of what it means to be part human, part animal. (That is, if meaning can be found in being, which will also be explored in some detail.) You should know that the forthcoming events are in no way examples of outright love and romanticism, but please feel free to interpret them however you wish. Unfortunately, due to hunger, not every creature will live. Those who do live to see tomorrow face a fierce battle with perpetual hollowness. Lastly, due to the inherent darkness of our setting, we'll all have to be vigilant and aware.

As they say in the theater, suspend your disbelief.
Otherwise, the reality of this world is very much like yours and mine.

Lewis swam. Faster, surely, than any person in the history of human personhood.

Of course, he wasn't a human. Nor was he fully shark. Yet.

Possessing only the memories of a former life, Lewis would learn the difference between loneliness and being alone.

And now here he was. Months of anticipation had led to this moment, a circumstance of vast unknowing. Lewis's vision clarified in the seawater. Variations of darkness extended for miles.

With a jolt: Lewis wanted to swim back to shore. He swam for miles along the coastline, but in the dark, he could not find the spot. Would Wren wait for him in case he changed his mind? Lewis realized it was all wrong. He'd made a terrible mistake, the worst of his life, telling Wren to go back to their home to continue their life without him in it, telling her it was impossible to create a new way of being together, being so sure Someone Else could help her wash the car and fix broken things in the house, sloughing off her grand plan to buy land, plant trees, have kids, build treehouses, and read plays beneath the stars. In his easy dismissal, he had erased a full range of possibilities. (Hadn't he been the dreamer, once, and she the skeptic?)

By daybreak, Lewis knew. Wren was gone.

Lewis reminded himself that this (*this:* what even was *this?*) was no fault of his own. He might spend days, months, years like *this*, alone. What a privilege it was to mark time with the sun.

THIS

On the drive to the ocean, Wren avoided the *R*-word, *release,* as if it were an insensitive slur. Lewis had his own *R*-word now.

REGRETS

He should have gotten a dog years ago.

He did not see enough David Lynch films, read Chekhov's short stories, or learn how to write songs. He should have been more present with the texture of fleece, the sensations of sweating and standing, the smells of grocery stores and ice cream shops, the tastes of glazed donuts and Brie, and the way his hair and fingernails grew without him even thinking about it.

He did not tell Wren how much he loved all her small things. The way her mouth dimpled on one side when she smiled; the way she took deep breaths when she did not know what to say or was trying not to laugh; her patience while explaining the stock market to him.

He never told his students the most transcendent theater performances he'd ever witnessed were theirs: moments when he was no longer their teacher but an imperfect man who had just apprehended a flash of enlightenment in the fourth row of the high school auditorium; moments when he was no longer a human becoming a shark, in fact: no longer a body at all but a celestial object, simultaneously born and dying from an overwhelm of love and goodness.

Most of all, Lewis wished he could tell his students that they transfigured his lonely ambition into a dream to change the world; how they were all artists of the highest caliber, fulfilling humankind's highest duty and delivering the message: faith lived in the darkest rooms.

On his second day in the ocean, Lewis felt an inward pull, an unfamiliar directional intuition, begging him to swim away from the coastal waters and westward into the open sea. As Lewis followed the tug, he irrationally expected to find something waiting for him, a welcoming home or a friendly greeter, but all he found was more of the same, deeper dark.

The ocean floor seemed as out of reach as the sun. At night, Lewis lingered so near the surface he could see the moon, a hazy pearlescent bulb. He still felt more comfortable with a blanket of oxygen near and above him. Lewis imagined it was summertime in their backyard pool, Wren floating beside him.

On the third day, Lewis tried to use his electroreception to find Wren's frequency, but all he picked up was a sea turtle a few meters away.

You are never really *alone,* his inner parent chimed in, to comfort him. But this time, the voice was wrong. Lewis was no longer a beloved family member or spouse; no longer at the helm of a theatrical ensemble; no longer a member of a society.

In this life, Lewis was a solitary animal.

On the fourth day, Lewis swam even deeper, tapping some primal courage in the void, which probably had something to do with his rapid growth since the release. Lewis grew a few inches every hour and had to eat constantly to meet his body's demands.

In deeper waters, suspended between here and there, Lewis kept both eyes open.

(Yes, of course, it was physiologically impossible for Lewis to close them, but also, he was terrified.)

I AM SO LONELY HERE, Lewis screamed and screamed and screamed and screamed and screamed and screamed. But no one heard him. No one came.

Lewis found no pleasure in his predatory nature, lacerating fish, squid, and smaller sharks. Instead, he harbored guilt about taking life from creatures who were, in comparison, so vulnerable and unlucky.

I wish I were an herbivore, Lewis thought as he feasted on tuna. Then he reconsidered. Plants were probably the most sentient of all living things: rational, bloodless bystanders, witnessing the great horror of it all.

Dear Wren,
This morning
I saw a sphere of color and light,
glowing blue and green.
Then I noticed them all around me, everywhere,
little topiary-like lanterns hovering in the water.
Jellyfish, I think?
I wish you could have seen it!
What a mistake I made,
letting you go.
In the rare hopeful hour, I tell myself this darkness has a purpose:
to help me recognize light if I ever find it again.
In the plethora of dismal times,
I will never forgive myself for leaving you,
alone.

Lewis missed time-shaping structures, like the weekend, holidays, business hours, and mealtimes. He missed toggling between creative projects. He even missed the quiet but brutal noise of the Internet. Now Lewis belonged, at once, to everywhere, nowhere, and no one.

Even with all this time, Lewis still couldn't bring himself to meditate.

Lewis capitulated to depression and then suicidal ideation.

He tried to starve himself to death, but eventually, his carnivorous impulse would override his cognitive desire to perish.

After each feeding, Lewis chastised himself and vowed, once more, to never eat again.

The cycle inevitably repeated. Lewis's self-loathing and frustration mounted.

If I still had my fists, Lewis grumbled to himself, *I would punch every damned thing.*

Then he met Margaret C. Finnegan.

Lewis felt her before he saw her: a strong, tingly circuit of energy flowed from the top of his head to his caudal fin, an intense electroreceptive recognition, a vibration stronger than heavy bass moving through his body at a concert. Instantly, Lewis knew he was approaching another like him, a great white shark who once was a human being.

"Stranger: can you understand me?" Her voice, a mezzo-soprano hum, had a metronomic quality not unlike the white noise of cicadas or frogs croaking with a biologically decided rhythm.

"Yes, I understand," Lewis replied, surprised to find that his oceanic vocal quality was the same as hers.

"Good. Hi."

"Hi."

"My name is Margaret C. Finnegan. And yours?"

(A pause when they would have shaken hands if they had hands.)

"Lewis Woodard."

"Hello, Lewis Woodard. Pleasure to make your acquaintance. How are you, sir?"

"I'm fine. And you?"

"I'm fine as well. In fact, today might be the best day I've ever seen here. Are you from North America, South America, Europe, or Asia?"

"Texas," Lewis said, realizing he sounded like one of those people who thought the Lone Star State was a country trapped within a nation.

"Where in Texas? I've been to the Alamo and SeaWorld San Antonio."

"Dallas."

"Oh, tell me! What is it like?"

"Well . . ." Lewis tried to summarize his former life's setting but could come up with only a few scattered particles:

"Inhumanely hot summers, but the winters are lovely. Big sky and endless grass. Enormous plates of Mexican food completely covered in cheese."

Margaret sighed longingly at his mention of cheese.

Lewis became suddenly very homesick. *If I was alone, I would cry,* he thought.

Out of necessity, Lewis accepted Margaret C. Finnegan as his companion. From the start, Lewis did not care for her personality—at all.

Margaret would not answer to anything but Margaret C. Finnegan in full, because her name was all she had left of her parents.

Also, she talked constantly.

And if Margaret wasn't talking, she was singing, and to Lewis's complete vexation, the only songs in her repertoire were snippets of three hits from the early 2000s ("Bootylicious," "Get Ur Freak On," and "Hot in Herre"), as well as Avril Lavigne's first two albums, which she knew by heart.

Margaret made Lewis recall his early days of student teaching, when he had a weak command of the classroom.

Lewis tried to catch her up on current events, but Margaret was most interested in what happened to the characters in a very specific mystery book series and which mammals were on or off the endangered species list.

To her great disappointment, Lewis was no help.

"Can I ask you a personal question?" Margaret asked.

"What is it?"

"How did people treat you when you were changing?"

Lewis thought of Wren, their day at the zoo, *Our Town,* The Ignoramus, his disastrous going-away party, the doctors, his parents.

"Carefully."

Margaret seemed to understand what he meant.

"Lewis Woodard, I want you to know I did some things I am not proud of."

SOME THINGS MARGARET B. FINNEGAN
IS NOT PROUD OF

Eating her mother's right ear. Margaret wasn't conscious during the act, but she remembered hours later listening, in horror, to her father recall the story.

Devouring the fish in her father's tropical fish aquarium, again forgetting the behavior that corresponded with being human.

Not saying goodbye, because she was too gone and weak to remember how.

Margaret C. Finnegan taught Lewis how to hunt seals. Lewis would play sidekick and eat what she killed, but he felt unbearable remorse attacking one by himself.

"How did you learn to hunt?" Lewis asked after they feasted on a couple of young seals, a meal that would last them for a few days.

"A dolphin pod found me when I was very sick and raised me with their own pups. When the pups were grown and ready to find their mates, they pushed me out."

"What did you do after that?"

"I went searching for my mate, too. And if you're here, there's got to be more of us. There has to be."

"I don't think so."

"Why?"

"Unlikely odds, I suppose, considering the size of the ocean."

"You have a very negative life outlook, Lewis Woodard."

"I'm a realist."

"No, you're an actor."

Dear Wren,
Would you believe the prattle-head Margaret C. Finnegan called me
a realist??
ME!
If only she knew
I am hopelessly dreaming
you and I
are in a long, mutual nightmare.
What do you say?
Let's start over. Let's wake up at the end of April.
Instead of getting bad news from Dr. Ramirez,
I'll learn it's all because of allergies or stress,
and in June, we'll go on our honeymoon, like we planned.
We'll spend all day in art museums,
picnic beneath the Eiffel Tower,
and tell each other
(with no knowledge of the alternative)
that all our dreams came true.

Margaret's roaming imagination and idealistic intensity made Lewis squirm, probably because these traits reminded him of himself. They were perhaps too alike to be fond of each other.

Lewis often thought he wanted to go out on his own. Other times, he knew he couldn't survive without her skills. Maybe even grating company like Margaret C. Finnegan was better than no company at all.

And then sometimes Margaret pushed Lewis into such a deep state of exasperation that her idiosyncrasies became a source of humor, and this humor developed into genuine pleasure, tricking Lewis into believing he enjoyed her company after all.

During those good and few times when the clouds parted, Margaret saw The Real Him. Lewis could be so funny and kind and generous and warm and handsome and thoughtful and caring, for someone who resented all aspects of living.

"Hey, Lewis?" Margaret asked in the tone of voice that preceded a pestering series of inquiries.

"What?"

"Can I ask you a personal question?"

"Depends."

"Do you believe in true love?"[1]

"No."[2]

---

1 Margaret C. Finnegan was developing a crush. She had never had a crush (only read about them), and she had only the object of her crush (Lewis) with whom to discuss the symptoms.

Margaret felt his smile was bright enough to turn the dark ocean aflame with light and colors yet to be seen or invented. Sometimes Margaret imagined them walking on land and holding hands. When they kissed, she would levitate to a place no girl has ever gone, a place no girl leaves.

She loved the dimple where Lewis still had the shadow of a human chin. She hoped he saw her the way she saw him.

2 Lewis's perspective on true love was more complicated than it used to be, thanks to his tumultuous year of marriage.

Truth and Love were complicated concepts on their own, and patching the two words together created a significant tangle Lewis could not unwind.

"**H**ey, Lewis?"
    "What?"
"Do you know what I've been thinking about?"
"What have you been thinking about."
"I haven't given up yet on finding others like us."
"You shouldn't waste your energy."
"Well, do you know how long I've been looking?"
"How long?"
"Guess."
"Just tell me."
"Please guess."
"No."
"Guess."
"Two months."
"Higher."
"Two years."
"Up."
"Three years."
"Longer."
"How long? Margaret. Just tell me."
"Twelve years, at the very minimum.
But I've lost track of some of the days,
so this guess is quite conservative.
It could be longer."
"You've been out here by yourself for twelve years?"
"Not the entire twelve years.
The dolphins for some.
But yes, mostly alone.
Except for part."
"Who were you with for the part that wasn't with the dolphins?"

"You."[1]

"How old are you?"

"Around twenty-four.

I think.

If I didn't miscount the days.

But twenty-four is my best guess.

I missed quite a few sunrises, especially early on.

I was very homesick.

And young.

I was released when I was thirteen.

How old are you, Lewis?"

"Thirty-five."

"Wow."

"What?"

"You're old."

"You're immature."

"Lewis:

if it hadn't been for me,

you would have died many times over.

You were helpless, frightened, and depressed when I found you.

You would've wasted away

only eating those little fish."

"I was not *helpless, frightened, and depressed,*" Lewis snapped, and decided never to tell Margaret he was trying to starve himself to death when she found him, and he couldn't even do that right.

---

1 The summer before sixth grade, Margaret went to the movies with a boy from youth group. They shared a large popcorn. Several times, their fingertips touched as they reached for the bucket, and when this happened, a galvanizing pulse thundered in her body.

Being around Lewis felt like one hundred times this.

"Lewis?"

"What?"

"Do you want to know what I've been thinking about?"

"What."

"The White Shark Café."

"Enough with that."

"It's somewhere between California and Hawaii. We could find it."

"Why would you want to?" Lewis asked, considering the reasons sharks would gather, feeding and breeding. He lurched at the thought of the latter.

"We could start a town. A place for people, sharks, like us. I know there are others."

"No, Margaret."

"Why not?"

"It doesn't work like that."

"How do you know?"

"We're perfectly fine without things and places. Things and places are how people live, and we are not people."

"Well, I disagree."

"Let's find the White Shark Café!" Margaret exclaimed at least twice a day for weeks, presenting it each time as if it were a new idea.

And each time, Lewis responded the same way:

"No."

Lewis dreamed he was the stem of a pear:

The pear was plopped in the water by a mystery hand from above,
and the leaves, winglike, were his arms, reaching upward.
If only I could fly, not swim, Lewis thought in the dream.
But the sweet weight of the pear anchored him.
And the more he struggled, the more he panicked, and the more he
panicked, the more he sank.

Periodically, Margaret would stop abruptly and make a timely, useful observation, interrupting her own chatter stream.

An example:

"One time, on a field trip, this boy in my class stuck a peanut up his nose, and the school bus had to take him to the emergency room, and while that was happening, another girl put a raisin up *her* nose and— OMG, Lewis: do you see the big shadow ahead?"

"Yeah, what is it?"

"A whale. We should turn around. Always remember: when it comes to whales, know your place, Lewis. It's never worth it in the end."

In ways like this, Margaret saved Lewis's life at least twice an hour.

A nd then the dominant, obnoxious-to-him side of Margaret C. Finnegan
would emerge again with full vigor:

"Lewis, could I ask you a personal question?"

"I don't know. Depends."

"Do you hate me?"

"Hate you?"

"Yeah."

"I don't hate you."

"Do you like me?"

"Why do you ask?"

"Well, Lewis, you should know a little something about me."

"What is that?"

. . .[1]

"What?"

"I think,

I think

maybe I love you."

"You *love* me? *Romantically?*" Lewis felt sick.

"I think I do, love you. Even though you're stubborn, grumpy, and
wholly unpleasant company: I confess I love you and have loved you,
strongly, since the first time I met you. What do you think about that?
Do you love me, too?"

---

1 Margaret considered telling Lewis any number of things instead of the truth bursting forth
from within her being. That she was cold. That she was warm. That she was tired. That she wasn't
cold, warm, or tired at all but wanted to ask if he was. That she'd just had a memory of a birthday
party she attended when she was six years of age. At this party, there was a birthday cake with
a Barbie doll lodged in the middle, so the cake appeared to be the skirt part of Barbie's dress.
The mom serving cake removed the Barbie to cut the cake, and because Margaret loved the
strawberry cream filling so very much, she took the Barbie when no one was looking. Holding
Barbie by her head and chest, Margaret began sweeping her tongue up and down Barbie's legs.
Margaret had no idea she was doing anything wrong when a mom yanked the Barbie from her
hands and barked, sternly, "Margaret, that is NOT appropriate behavior." She felt embarrassed
for years and years and never understood why.

"Margaret. I'm a married man. You know this."

"You *were*. You left her on the beach in California, remember?" Margaret jabbed, knowing just how and where to hurt him.

Each felt wronged by the other. Margaret for being rejected and Lewis for being accused of leaving Wren on purpose; he regretted telling Margaret anything about her.

"Well, I suppose that's goodbye, Lewis. I was perfectly fine before I met you. It's you who weren't fine. Don't come to me when you are hungry. Don't come to me when the seasons change and you need to learn the migratory pattern. Don't call for my help when you get caught by fishermen. And you can't admit it, but you know you're a terrible predator without me."

Then Margaret darted away in a fury. Lewis watched her flutter away, recalling the last time a woman left him alone in the ocean. Both times he was passive. Both times he felt euphoric and then promptly forlorn.

Lewis stopped marking the days, and they blurred into one another as they had before he met Margaret.

Exiled from the plane of conversation and things and doing and going and seeking and becoming, Lewis simply existed.

Sometimes Lewis thought he saw famous earthly landmarks in the distance: the Statue of Liberty, the Golden Gate Bridge, the Delicate Arch. When he got closer, it would be a boat, a reef, seaweed, a mass of floating trash, or nothing at all. Once Lewis thought he saw Wren swimming toward him, and he bolted ahead, swimming as fast as he could to meet her.

Wren is here! She is looking for me! he thought.

But each time, it was only a wishful ripple in his memory.

Dear Wren,
I used to have romantic notions about being alone in nature.
In practice, it is entirely trying.
If you must know,
trying is all I do.
Try to eat.
Try not to be eaten.
Try not to think,
especially of you.

Lewis often replayed the Masterpiece Memory, his vestige of comfort, the night Wren and strawberry moon became a part of the same wholeness. Lewis tried to remember every thread, wrinkle, scent, and freckle.

> hair splayed behind her
> that small, restful smile
> cutoff shorts
> the T-shirt from one of the spring musicals
> Was it *Little Shop of Horrors*?
> Or had it been *Sweeney Todd*?
> And then Wren's face—
> her face—
> her face—
> *her face—!*

Wren's face was gone.

Lewis could not remember her face.

Lewis churned through his mind, trying to find a fragment of her, but not a single freckle, eyelash, or finger appeared. Could the picture of Wren's face in his mind really be gone? Did memories decompose?

Then the entire Masterpiece Memory slipped from Lewis's mind, like an escaped helium balloon floating toward the clouds. Afterward, he could remember only the memory of the memory. Lewis was devastated.

This is a ridiculous thing to be sad about, Lewis thought, and cried anyway.

To become a great white shark is to become well acquainted with paradox: The timeline of his life which once felt so linear now contained an excruciating number of options and, at the same time, none.

How could Lewis fear his physical death when his thoughts and memories were shape-shifting, dissolving into a place unknown?

And without thoughts and memories, what was the man called Lewis Woodard? Nothing. But even nothing was something.

Death could happen now or in two hundred years. Lewis did not care as much as he once did about his life, much less its course, the contents of his days.

Lewis discovered a layer of sadness even deeper than his previous depression: a bleak, gorgeous fog so quiet and still it resembled peace.

As Lewis existed in this underworld of exceptional sorrow, something strange and incredible began to happen, seemingly against his will. He had plunged into such psychological darkness that he began to see glimmers of its opposite, light.

Lewis would catch himself enjoying pleasant moods and tranquil states until he reminded himself that he was supposed to be uniquely and unwaveringly depressed.

Eventually, Lewis was able to laugh, even marvel, at his own absurdities:

I am a great white shark with mental health struggles!
I am a great white shark who knows Shakespeare!
I am a great white shark haunted by regret!
I am a great white shark who misses fruit!
I am a great white shark who speaks English!
I am a great white shark who's been to the Grand Canyon!
I am a great white shark who will never forgive myself for leaving my wife!

Gradually, Lewis's inner alignment began to self-correct.

He would recall the process when he was on the other side and puzzle over the miracle.

Was it magic that saved my life? Lewis wondered as he devoured a sea lion with no remorse. *Or was my suffering just an ordinary dip, a developmental phase that was always meant to pass with time?*

For the first time since he'd arrived in the ocean, Lewis's mind and body were in the same place.

He not only missed Margaret, he also understood—and shared!—her hope and longing for community.

So, maybe love wasn't an unwieldy accessory in times of peril. Maybe it was the key to survival.

Lewis went looking for Margaret
along reefs and migrations
through storms
and along coastlines
past plastic pollution
beneath broad white sterns.
Bypassing fishing boats and divers with cameras
who gazed at him with curiosity and fear through thick goggles,
frenzied reactions to his every movement.
Lewis swam onward, looking, hoping, and remembering.
Margaret's singing
and her regrets:
mother's ear, father's fish, feeble goodbyes.
Dolphin cubs,
hunting strategies,
a preoccupation with the White Shark Café,
her unwavering commitment to civilization.

On this search, Lewis sensed a whale birth from afar, tasting traces of blood in the water. At first, he resisted his impulse to follow it to the source. Lewis was not consciously bloodthirsty, but the fresh afterbirth enlivened him in a way he could not control.

Lewis put aside Margaret's advice: *When it comes to whales, know your place, Lewis. It's never worth it in the end.*

The squirming calf was pillow-soft, a delicacy, his best feeding since Margaret left.

Lewis jettisoned the carcass, letting it drift toward the ocean floor.

Later, as Lewis tried to outswim three orcas, he understood Margaret's warning. Lewis was indicted for a crime he did indeed commit, and unless he could find a way to evade his predators, he would pay with his own life.

Lewis realized he did not fear death but grief, the ache of being alone and mangled by change. Yet he was not ready to make peace with the end. Lewis had something, someone, to live for.

While the calf's mother led the attack on him, Lewis swam as fast as he could, beseeching God, his old pal, whose whole thing, it seemed, was about being amorphous and inconsistent at best.

Margaret, a miracle bursting through the darkness, fought the whales so Lewis could swim away.

"GO, GO, GO!" she screamed. "I'll find you!"

Cries. Blood filled the water. Hers. And his. Time stretched. Lewis lost consciousness, surrendering again to the dark and Margaret's familiar presence.

Their blood formed red tributaries around their bodies. They were alive, barely. But still, alive.

Lewis and Margaret healed their bodies and passed their time, telling stories of past lives.

Lewis told Margaret stories about Wren (well, what he had left)—

hair splayed
that smile
cutoffs
Little Shop of Horrors
a strawberry moon
his wife, his life

who at times seemed like a character in a wonderful book, a static entity whose movements, while profound, would always be limited to a finite story.

Margaret told Lewis stories about her best friends. (They were girls when Margaret began her mutation, and it ripped Margaret apart to think about how they had all become women without her.)

Sophie
Maria
Lily
Naomi
and Anna, Margaret's "best *best* friend,"
whom she missed most of all.

"Me and Anna were on a Girl Scout camping trip, and this one night we snuck out of our tents 'cause Anna really, *really* wanted to see a shooting star. And we did! And afterward, we decided right then and there to be sisters for eternity. Both of us being only children and all."

"I was an only child, too," Lewis replied.

SCENE: A Giant

LEWIS: I used to
   act
   write
   teach
   I wanted to be a Giant.
   But maybe I should have just been
   me.

MARGARET: Tell me the story of the play you wrote. Act it out.

LEWIS: I don't remember any of it.

MARGARET: Well, that's too bad. I'm bored and would like to hear a story.

. . .

LEWIS: Margaret, we don't need to find the White Shark Café. Let's make a town right here, right now.

MARGARET: Really? You mean it?

LEWIS: I've been thinking lately,
    maybe we do get new performances of the same day,
    opportunities to be more accepting and loving.
    Maybe practice, rehearsal, is also the way to freedom.
    We can start over.
    Time can loop back on itself,
    and here I am again
    with you, Margaret,
    trying.

. . .

MARGARET: I have literally no idea what you are talking about.

Because the migratory urge was quite present in each of them, Margaret and Lewis decided their town should not be bound by a physical location.

"What if the town is made of *stories*?" Margaret suggested in a crisp lightbulb moment, the kind of perfect and complete idea Lewis knew came only a few times in a lifetime.

From that moment on, the project became clear.

As Lewis and Margaret went about their days together, they added familiar and imagined places, people both living and dead, and thanks to Margaret, a myriad of elves, unicorns, and incarnations of every American Girl doll.

"I think the town should have a Blockbuster. A Blockbuster where everything is free," Margaret said with a ping of excitement.

Lewis considered telling her Blockbuster was gone, too, another casualty of time and change.

"Sounds good to me," he replied.

Gradually, Lewis began to accept that this was the life he wanted to be living, simply because it was the only life he had. Margaret and Lewis got better at existing together, walking the same uncommon tightrope, dividing the worlds of humans and beasts.

"You know what?" Margaret said as they feasted on rays off the western coast of Kauai.

"What's that?"

"You're like a brother to me."

Lewis felt his fins tingle as a light flickered on in him, his retired boyhood wish for a sibling coming to life.

"You're like a sister to me," Lewis echoed, realizing as he said it that few things had ever felt so true.

They both stopped swimming to look at each other, glassy eye to glassy eye.

"Would you like to be family?" Lewis asked slowly, not because he was unsure but because he had nothing to offer her but his self and his time.

"A *family*?"

"Yes."

"Like, brother and sister?" asked Margaret.

"You and me."

"Family," Margaret said again, this time through tears. "I thought it would never happen to me."

Even though his quality of life improved, Lewis's inner turmoil about Wren never diminished. The ache felt like a material object lodged inside him, and while he could momentarily distract himself from its presence, the pain was always with him.

Lewis and Margaret saw scuba divers, once near Monterey and another time between Maui and Lanai.

The third time, Margaret swam toward the open ocean while Lewis lingered too close, checking for Wren, frightening the divers. If he found Wren, Lewis did not know what he would do to show her he was still Lewis Woodard, her long-ago love. She probably would not recognize him now that he had outgrown all his human features. Lewis wondered if he still had the same essence. And if he did, would that be enough?

"It wasn't her. Let's go on," Lewis reported when he rejoined Margaret.

"You know what, Lewis?"

"What."

Margaret knew about Wren's mother, Angela, her mutation, the house-boat, the lake, and the small country house. She knew all about Wren's absent, peripatetic father who ended up in prison for car theft, Wren's grandmother Colleen who had three husbands but met Wren only once, and her grandpa Rick who helped with money throughout her childhood but died of a heart attack on a golf course when Wren was fourteen. Margaret knew Wren could do perfect math in her head. She knew Wren went to an Ivy League college but hated saying so because she didn't want to make anyone feel unequal. She knew Wren had about eleven different ways to laugh, but when something was deeply funny, she laughed in a way that made no sound at all. She knew how Wren felt about Mother's Day, clutter, and the wedding industry. She knew Wren was a perfectionist not because she wanted to be but because she felt she had to be to survive in an unfair world. Margaret knew that Wren left her job to take care of Lewis and filled an aboveground pool in the backyard with saltwater so he would be more comfortable as he was transforming. She knew Wren walked the

378

neighborhood when she could not sleep. She knew Wren wanted to be a mother one day. Margaret knew Lewis gave her his blessing to begin again.

"Lewis, you've told me so much about Wren, sometimes I think I miss her, too. She would want you to be happy. She would want you to find joy."

"Is that everything?" Lewis replied as the knot in his stomach got caught in his throat.

"For now."

JOY

DECEMBER

After more travel through the Southwest, Wren returned home to Dallas. She had nowhere else to be. The city's friendly sterility was no longer comforting, and the ribbons of stacked serpentine highways on either side of her neighborhood seemed strange and artificial now.

To survive each endless day, Wren made lists of chores and forced herself to complete them.

She vacuumed all the difficult places (beneath and behind the washer and dryer, behind bookshelves, the impossibly narrow cracks in the car).

She threw away Lewis's medication, toiletries, and hot sauce collection.

She rearranged the furniture in the living room to disrupt her haunted memories of the space, pushing the sofa against a wall that didn't make sense, which meant she had to climb over the sofa to open the patio door.

She slept in the guest room on new, cheap sheets.

She painted the living room a color named Agreeable Gray and hated it immensely.

Each day, Wren found herself saying internally that she couldn't imagine a life without him, and yet here she was, living it.

Wren continued to find treehouse drawings all over the house, but she avoided the draft of Lewis's play, an unbound stack of papers held together with a thick binder clip, atop his bedroom bookshelf.

She thought carefully about what to do with this sacred text and decided to read only a single word each day. She paced herself, maintaining this word diet for almost two weeks. But one night, after treating herself to two sentences, she binged the whole play.

Wren was disgusted with herself and then devastated. His work could no longer be discovered. She had lost him all over again.

On the day Wren planned to return to work, an ice storm shut down all of North Texas. Wren couldn't bear being alone in the house for a moment longer.

She walked the perimeter of the backyard a few times, crunching on frozen grass, and collapsed into the frozen hammock. The ice snapped and fell off in frozen ropes beneath her. The last time she was there, it was summer, Lewis's body pressed against her own.

A murmuration of blackbirds settled in waves: on the roof, on the telephone lines, in the tree, on the frosted grass. The blackbirds kept coming, getting closer and closer to the hammock, crowding one another, and blanketing the backyard until no space was untouched except Wren and the hammock.

Then, as quickly as they settled, the birds tilted their selfish onyx eyes to the sky and levitated as a single segmented unit. It seemed nothing, not even the birds, was meant to stay beside her very long. It seemed she was just the sort of person who repelled lasting connection. It seemed loving someone was not enough to keep them still beside her.

Feverish, surprising laughter exited her body. Wren howled at the absurdity of her rare odds, the suffering, the sacrifice. Then an unexplained stillness overcame her. Wren thought of her lungs' thin membranes, pumping oxygen for over thirty-five years without taking a break, the frailty of her joints and bones, and her eyeballs, these fragile mystery-meat globs that contained a complicated mechanism for sight, everything she ever knew. Lewis and Wren had met in a daydream, once, but they had also known each other in real life.

Who am I supposed to be without you? she asked Lewis in her head.

Anything you like, he replied.

Wren called up to the bird quartet lingering on the tree branch above her: "I am an animal, too, you know."

JANUARY

Unexpectedly, Wren was pregnant.

Given Wren's family history, the genetic counselor said, the fetus, while human now, would remain high-risk for animal mutation throughout its lifetime.

Wren texted the Tiny Pregnant Woman using the excuse of checking in. Really, Wren wanted company. She wanted to be near someone who understood her lonely predicament. When the Tiny Pregnant Woman did not respond, Wren had the thought to google her, even though she feared what she might learn. An obituary came up first in the search results.

> *Nora Clifton, 33, of Dallas, Texas, went to be with the Lord on December 3, 2016, after complications in childbirth. She was a daughter, wife, and mother and, once, a decorated young swimmer.*

Wren could not bring herself to read the rest.

For days after the appointment, Wren found herself staring into spreadsheet voids at work, trying to imagine what Lewis would say.

Was it ethical to create life knowing this person could suffer from such a cruel and painful condition? Would she be able to bear losing a child in the same way she'd lost her mother and husband? How could a family find happiness with the possibility of tragedy always lurking in future times? Wren decided to terminate the pregnancy.

The night before the abortion, Wren woke at three o'clock in the morning trapped in sweat-soaked sheets. She walked the neighborhood until dawn, Lewis's words repeating like a song lyric stuck in her head.

You will be a wonderful mother.
You will be a wonderful mother.
You will be a wonderful mother.
You will be a wonderful mother.
You will be a wonderful mother.
You will be a wonderful mother.
You will be a wonderful mother.

Later that morning, Wren canceled the appointment.

Meanwhile, a chain of genetic material from each of the people Wren most loved swirled within the small being Wren would love most of all.

FEBRUARY

Wren was grieving and falling madly in love at the same time, which created a new, wild corridor in her personality. In one moment, Wren was furious at Lewis, life, and herself. In another, she entered an inexplicable, overwhelming peace.

In these waves of contentment, Wren became the kind of person who would tell the morning sun she appreciated its consistency and the one-time-nemesis armadillo digging for the grubs in the backyard at dusk, *Welcome back.*

MARCH

When she felt the baby move, Wren would give anything to reach for Lewis's hand and guide it to the spot on her body where life had just begun.

APRIL

Wren was having a girl, and she could not stop smiling. She smiled at the office. She smiled when she was alone. She smiled even as she cried. For the first time, she did not want to be invisible in the world. People smiled back.

The obvious choice emerged. Wren decided to name her daughter Angela, after her mother.

MAY

Holding her daughter for the first time, Wren abruptly changed her mind. This was Joy.

Joy, six months

As her personality emerges, Wren, Annie, and Greg often look at one another with the same bewildered, teary-eyed expression. They wonder, each in their own way, if some part of Lewis's spirit is coming through to animate this new, seraphic being.

Joy, age one

Wren looks down at her phone for three seconds, and while she is distracted, Joy almost puts a fistful of an ant colony in her mouth.

Wren learns she can't look away for a moment, and really, that's fine with her. She doesn't want to miss a thing.

Joy, age two

Joy loves nothing more than being pushed in a swing. She is fearless. (*Higher, higher, higher,* Joy says.) And the higher she goes, the more she laughs, and Joy has the best laugh. While she smiles and cackles, she kicks her gooey legs and extends her arms like she's expecting a hug from the sky.

Joy is a little girl who has no qualms about taking the space she needs with her voice, physicality, and huge emotions. Wren realizes she has much to learn from her.

Joy, age three

In the spring, the pandemic grasps the world, and the frightened, cabin-fevered people look to nature for relief. But Joy is already outside. From sunup to sundown, Joy meets the outdoors with bare feet in the grass and hands in the dirt. She is one of those kids who, when set free in a park or backyard, becomes impervious to cold, hunger, and time.

Joy, age four

She prefers to wear the next day's clothes to bed instead of pajamas so she can run outdoors first thing in the morning unencumbered by the process of getting dressed for the day.

Late summer, Joy captures huge grasshoppers in her cupped palms, not to torture or dissect them but to briefly love them, as a friend, and set them free with a whisper, *Fly home now. Fly home!*

Joy, age five

Joy learns to climb trees, and Wren has never been more consumed with circumstantial anxiety.

"Can we pleeeeeeeeeease build a treehouse?" Joy begs Wren one evening after the nanny leaves. A memory of Lewis drawing treehouse blueprints in the same chair where her daughter now sits flashes in Wren's mind.

"I'll think about it," Wren says, pushing down the swell of grief. "Go wash your hands for dinner. Thirty seconds. And soap!"

The next day, Wren tells her therapist about Joy's treehouse question.

"What is coming up for you?" the therapist asks.

Wren struggles to speak. The therapist tells Wren to take her time.

"Lewis,

                                        he would have loved—

                Lewis would love—

                      all

                              of

                                      this."

Joy, age six

Wren and Joy go up to Oklahoma when the weather is nice and teach themselves how to thrive in the wild. The natural world becomes both a mystery and a home.

In nature, Wren realizes she is becoming more like her mother and thinks, *How wonderful.*

At work, Wren begins to speak in metaphors and realizes she is becoming more like Lewis. This is wonderful, too.

At home, Joy inspires an alchemic shift in Wren's perspective. Wren no longer sees life as a long, linear ladder with a beginning, middle, and end. Instead, she considers how life is like a spiraling trail up a mountain. Each circling lap represents a learning cycle, the same lesson at a slightly higher elevation. Wren realizes she likes to rest as much as she likes to climb. She begins to enjoy the view.

On Christmas Eve, Joy falls asleep beneath the tree, watching *Elf.*

"Is it morning? Did Santa come?" Joy asks, groggy. She is all limbs now, almost too gangly to carry to bed.

"No, it's still night. Santa won't come until you're sleeping in your bed."

"Okay . . ."

When Wren returns to the living room to arrange the presents, she's shaken by the energy of love radiating out of and beyond her body. This love expands until it fills the entire room, house, neighborhood, city, nation, planet, and the universe, beyond.

Afterward, Wren realizes she herself is the mountain she's been climbing all along.

Joy, age seven

After a summer of camping, Joy begs Wren to let her camp in the backyard for a night. Joy also wants a dog, a black Labrador like their neighbor's.

Wren says no to the dog (for now) but succumbs to the pressure of backyard camping. Joy is thrilled. This becomes their Saturday-night ritual until it gets chilly at night.

Joy has so many questions. She wants to know the names and reasons for everything. She learns to identify clouds from YouTube and watches the same documentary about space until she has the host's lines memorized.

Somehow, without trying, Joy contains each of her parents' best qualities: Wren's precision and intellectualism. Lewis's ability to wonder and dream.

Joy, age eight

Now Joy's curiosity turns its gaze toward who her father was as a person. Each night before bed, Joy asks a question about him, and Wren must produce a corresponding story. At first, Wren thinks she will run out of stories but realizes early in the project that she actually has an expansive supply.

"Can we go to a play, like my dad?" Joy asks after Wren tells her about Lewis's twenties in New York.

"Yes, but you'll have to sit still and be very quiet for a long time." Wren says, remembering the first play she attended with Lewis, an unabridged production of *Richard III*.

"I can do it," Joy says, determined.

These echoes of Lewis in Joy used to choke Wren. Now they make her feel lucky.

Joy, age nine

On a warm weekend in early March, Wren rents a canoe to show Joy how to paddle. Wren sits at the stern, where Angela once sat, and Joy takes her position at the bow, where Wren had as a girl.

With her mother's strength behind her, Joy glimpses her power, gliding through the water into an undiscovered frontier, at the helm of a whole wide world. Joy, with her ancestors residing within her like nesting dolls, is a brave, flaming heart, born to face the wound of the world, and one day she will be one among the wave to heal it.

"Mom!" Joy whisper-shouts, turning abruptly and dropping her paddle. "Look up!"

A bald eagle soars above them, a fierce angel swooping low—just a couple dozen feet from their heads.

Then Joy does the single thing you're not supposed to do in a canoe. She stands up.

Joy, age ten

For Joy's spring break, Wren plans a road trip down the California coastline. They rent a car at the airport in San Francisco and camp at Big Sur. They will stay a night in Santa Barbara before cruising the PCH to Anaheim for a surprise finale at Disneyland.

After Big Sur, they start passing familiar signs for Morro Bay. Wren's chest tightens. She had thought about this moment when she was planning the trip, passing the place where she and Lewis said goodbye over ten years ago. Wren cannot resist its pull.

Joy has no idea this is the place, the end, and for now, Wren decides to keep it that way.

"Not too deep! Stay in the shallow where you can touch!" Wren calls out as Joy sprints toward the water.

As Joy splashes in the surf, Wren speaks quietly to the wind, a wind she hopes will carry her message, like light waves to another galaxy, across the sea, to Lewis.

"Well, here I am,
doing what you told me,
surviving,
existing,

beginning again.
Your work has a life of its own now,
extending beyond
time
chaos
me.
The last time we were here,
I thought I had nothing left.
But you had already given me the world.
I just didn't know it yet.
Everything is different.
I don't think you'd recognize me."

An angled beam of sunlight streams through the cumulonimbus clouds suspended above the sea.

Joy stands back, watching a pair of surfers paddle out past the wave break. Wren senses her daughter's longing to swim far out; to cast aside her mother's notion of risk; to touch as much of the world as possible.

"In some ways, she is like me:
good with numbers,
reads every direction,
a listener.
But mostly, Joy is like you.
She found your shelf of plays, and now we read them aloud together.
You will be pleased to know we started with Chekhov.
Like you, she wants to play the most complicated characters.
Like you, she has a huge smile that lights up her whole face
and the world, too.
Like you, she has a bountiful, brilliant imagination,
spending all day in her treehouse,
creating myths,
making friends,
sleeping hard.

And then there are the ways she is not like either of us.

I named her Joy before I knew what she would do to me.

Maybe life is a little magic after all.

There can be no other way to explain it."

Joy runs up to Wren, blue-lipped and shivering.

"Mom! Come swim! It's not cold at all!"

A few minutes later, Wren stands at the edge of the surf.

"Just take it one step at a time. I promise you'll get used to it." Joy demonstrates, running ahead until she is waist-deep. "You have to be brave."

"I'm not brave. Not like you," Wren says.

"It's only cold at first."

Joy runs back to shore and webs her fingers through her mother's. They wade out together, squealing and jumping when a wave passes through them. When they are deep enough, Joy counts to seven, her favorite number, and together, they go under. The ocean is frigid and rough, and for a second, Wren can't think of anything but cold. Then the familiar flood of fear—

Wren squeezes the small hand she cannot protect from heartbreak, tragedy, or mutation. The small hand who made her selfless; who taught her there were no guarantees in love; who showed her for every sleepless night, supermarket tantrum, and smear of mud on the carpet, there are a thousand other things:

Joy gripping the armrest during the opening of the *Lion King* musical. Watching a sunset together in the fall at Quartz Mountain. Joy's face when she discovers the treehouse George and his son built in the backyard while she was away at camp, Lewis's exact design. Surprising Joy with a Labrador puppy on the last day of second grade. Wren, suppressing her laughter when Joy decides to name it Uncle Vanya.

Yes! Yes! Yes! Yes! Yes! Wren wants to shout. The world is a big and small place, and life, a terrifying and sublime journey.

Their heads break through the surface just as a bigger wave threatens to tear them apart.

The small hand wants to pull away from her mother's safe hold. The small, dear hand needs to swim, explore, love. The ocean cannot be contained; neither can love; neither can Joy. Wren loosens her grasp. It is so hard to let go.

"Go, play, be free," Wren says, heart hammering like rain on a metal roof.

Joy somersaults into a wave, disappears for a second, and emerges, smiling.

"It's easy. See?"

Acknowledgments

Shark Heart exists today because of an astounding web of support and collaboration. My gratitude feels immeasurable and indescribable, but I will try to express what I can, here.

Thank you to my literary agent, Sarah Bedingfield, for her advocacy, guidance, and faith in me, my ideas, and this book. Thank you also to my editor, Marysue Rucci, a dream creative partner whose genius insight made *Shark Heart* so much better. Marysue and Sarah, each with tremendous talent and wisdom, shared a bright vision for my unusual book and made my first publication process both a pleasure and profound privilege.

Much gratitude to the masterminds who contributed their creative and logistical skills and supported the book's journey in countless ways: Jiaming Tang at Marysue Rucci Books; Kyle Kabel, Jaya Micelli, Heather Musika, Vi-An Nguyen, Jessica Preeg, Nan Rittenhouse, Wendy Sheanin, and Laura Wise at Simon & Schuster; Kate Lloyd at Kate Lloyd Literary; Courtney Paganelli, Cristela Henriquez, Melissa Rowland, and Kirsten Wolf at Levine Greenberg Rostan Literary Agency; Will Watkins and Randie Adler at CAA.

Thank you to the following people who spoke candidly with me about their lived and professional experiences, enriching aspects of the novel about which I knew little: Bridget Bechtel for allowing me to glimpse inside her professional life as woman in finance; Abby Siegal Hyman for sharing her perspectives on new motherhood; Joy Hyman for inspiring Wren's daughter; Meg Scruggs for opening my eyes to the nuance and heartbreak in family law; Dr. Gregory Skomal for sharing his expertise on great white sharks and for creating *The Shark Handbook: The Essential Guide for Understanding the Sharks of the World,* which ignited my imagination in the research stage and increased my empathy for sharks as often misunderstood animals.

Thank you to my teacher and friend, Victor Judge, for the gift of his rare, transformative pedagogy and for demonstrating a vocational life in the service of souls and art.

Thank you to the many playwrights that have inspired me, including Thornton Wilder's *Our Town*, a work that is among my greatest teachers.

For their brilliant ideas, inspiration, advice, and unwavering support of my writing life, I owe much to Susan Baldwin, Curtis Baxter, Martha Collings, Celesta Edwards, Seraphina Nova Glass, Elizabeth Green, John Paul Green, Elizabeth Welliver Hengen, Mary Izzo, Sean LaLiberte, Camillia McDonald, Whitney Salinas, Rachel Cooley Shawler, Kevin Slane, Grace Talusan, Chanel Vidal, and Lauren Zbylski.

Thank you to my siblings, Katherine Habeck and John Habeck, for dreaming with me, challenging me, and inspiring me by forging their own paths.

Thank you to Max for his optimism, tenderness, and steadfast belief in my work; for being the world's best listener when I need to talk through a story idea at almost any hour of the day or night; for understanding my compulsion to write as a thing both part of me and beyond me.

Most importantly, I am grateful and fortunate to have parents who believe that a career in the arts is an entirely reasonable proposition. In my girlhood, my father nurtured my interest in theater and adopted my passion as his own. In the fallow seasons of my adult years, he was invariably inspiriting, reminding me that no experience is wasted and that big things take time. My mother, the most prolific reader I know and a natural dramaturg, was the first person to read *Shark Heart*, and she improved countless drafts through the years. I will forever cherish the afternoons we spent sitting at the dining room table with hundreds of pages between us, going through her notes.

When I write of a mother's love, I write not from the experience of being one myself but from being a daughter who has been so, so lucky to be loved by parents like you.